In an effort no[t]
her gaze slipp[ed]

...to his lips. Another strategic mistake. Luke's mouth was surely sweet to the touch. Full round lips...alluringly sensual. Addictive... *Yes.* Mr. Winter most definitely had an air of sexuality.

No way was he a nice guy. He had bad boy, hot nights and great orgasms written all over him. Tempting, spicy, delicious, but not nice. Never nice. And it was exactly what Katie was looking for....

Suddenly, everything else dropped away and there was only Luke before her. Tension, entwined with attraction, exploded. Heat pooled low in her belly, her heart pounded deeply in her chest. Slowly, their eyes met and it was one of *those* moments, when the look between a man and a woman is about to mean wild, passionate sex.

Blaze

Dear Reader,

What can I say? I love a hot baseball player, so it's no wonder one keeps finding his way into my books! And there is something so extra special and sexy about a pitcher. The way he controls the mound. The way he controls the game. The way he wears those tight pants. You get the picture!

When writing *Hot Target,* I loved the idea of pitcher Luke Winter having control, but giving it to his heroine, Katie Lyons, to earn her trust despite a past heartbreak. The path to that trust, however, isn't simple. It's slow, sexy and yes, dangerous. After all, not only is there a stalker on the loose, there are hearts to mend. Eventually, those hearts know where to run, and it isn't to first base. It's all the way home for the biggest score of all: love!

I hope you enjoy the romance. Please visit my Web site at www.lisareneejones.com for updates on my new Blaze trilogy coming in 2011!

Happy reading!

Lisa Renee Jones

Lisa Renee Jones

HOT TARGET

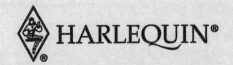

TORONTO • NEW YORK • LONDON
AMSTERDAM • PARIS • SYDNEY • HAMBURG
STOCKHOLM • ATHENS • TOKYO • MILAN • MADRID
PRAGUE • WARSAW • BUDAPEST • AUCKLAND

Recycling programs
for this product may
not exist in your area.

ISBN-13: 978-0-373-79563-5

HOT TARGET

ABOUT THE AUTHOR

Lisa spends her days writing the dreams playing in her head. Before becoming a writer, Lisa lived the life of a corporate executive, often taking the red-eye flight out of town and flying home for the excitement of a Little League baseball game. Visit Lisa at www.lisareneejones.com.

Books by Lisa Renee Jones

HARLEQUIN BLAZE
339—HARD AND FAST
442—LONE STAR SURRENDER

HARLEQUIN NOCTURNE
THE BEAST WITHIN
BEAST OF DESIRE
BEAST OF DARKNESS

Don't miss any of our special offers. Write to us at the following address for information on our newest releases.

Harlequin Reader Service
U.S.: 3010 Walden Ave., P.O. Box 1325, Buffalo, NY 14269
Canadian: P.O. Box 609, Fort Erie, Ont. L2A 5X3

To Matthew and Ronald for giving me so many reasons to enjoy baseball. To Diego for giving me so much encouragement and love. And to Janice for helping me make each book better.

Prologue

EVEN SEX HAD lost its appeal.

And damn if he thought he would ever see that day. But the simple fact was—sex now came with too many hidden agendas.

Gone were the days when sex was just sex, two people's mutual desire to share their bodies, a release that came with pleasure and maybe some sincere emotion if it was with the right person.

He let out a disgusted snort.

Who was the last woman he was with who hadn't thought he was a score because he was a pitcher in the majors? He couldn't even remember. The less naive he'd become, the more he had looked back at the past and realized there had been a lot of bull in most of his adult relationships.

Luke Winter stood behind the mahogany wet bar in the far corner of the basement-level den of his Los Angeles home. It was his room of peace, the place he always chose to unwind and embrace being by himself, a sanctuary of sorts.

A place where he pretended to be normal.

But he wasn't normal or he wouldn't be getting death threats from a crazy fan. No, he was a pro baseball player, a pitcher even. He had it all.

Or so everyone thought.

An old television hung from the ceiling, just above the bar, even though a massive big-screen sat in the center of the room. Luke never wanted to miss a major sporting moment because he was across the room. He needed to see the action up close and personal.

Leaning his palms against the railing of the bar, he struggled to stay focused on the television. It was April twenty-sixth, and the Texas Rangers were playing their last preseason game, which normally would have held his interest. He had a special fondness for several of their players. After all, he'd played, side by side, with them for years.

He'd never forget the day he'd gotten the call, the day he was told he was going to the big leagues, pitching for the Rockets. Even years after, and two teams later, playing for the California Hawks, he still loved the Rockets.

Yet today, his mind lingered on the upcoming meeting that his manager had arranged with some security specialist.

Katie Lyons.

A woman.

Why had he agreed to meet her? He wasn't even slightly inclined to agree to extra security. What he really wanted was to be left the hell alone.

What was making him so dissatisfied with life in general? Most people would kill for what he had. Of course, very few understood the things that were lost when you were in the public eye.

He stared in the direction of the television without really seeing it, absentmindedly tapping a finger on the bar.

An impending feeling of capriciousness had consumed his thoughts the majority of the day. He hated feeling as if he didn't have control over his own existence. Feeling out of sorts, he ran one hand roughly through his hair.

He was known as a nice guy. Well, damn it, maybe that was his problem. He was a walking target. Maybe taking back control would put an end to his sense of dissatisfaction.

Katie Lyons would be the first to witness a new Luke. He didn't want extra security, plain and simple. So he'd make sure this Katie Lyons hated him so much she not only refused the job, but ran all the way home.

1

LEAVE IT to a man to get a woman in trouble.

Katie Lyons gritted her teeth just thinking of the loser husband her sister had once hooked up with and had now dumped.

Just not soon enough.

Kyle Rogers, the low-down, scum-of-the-earth jerk, had hooked her younger sister, Carrie, on gambling to the tune of fifty thousand dollars, which Carrie had proceeded to ask Katie for as flippantly as if it were a cup of sugar.

Though Lyons Security was doing well, it had only opened a year ago when, at thirty, she'd decided it was now or never, and she'd taken the plunge. And financially, it was indeed a plunge. Fifty thousand dollars was like asking for water in a desert.

It wasn't happening.

Only it had to happen or Carrie's health and well-being would be in jeopardy. Because some wrestler-looking dude kept showing up at all hours of the night, threatening to use the baseball bat he carried around with him to influence Carrie's pocketbook.

Katie sighed heavily and shoved a long lock of her straight brunette hair behind her ear as she followed her old friend Ron Mortan through the foyer of Luke Winter's house.

Ron turned to look at her. "You okay?"

Katie forced a smile. "As fine as I can be, considering I let you talk me into this in the first place. You know how I feel about working for athletes."

"You don't know what it's like to work *with* an athlete. You dated Joey, you didn't work for him." His expression held just a hint of reprimand.

Katie's lips tightened. "I saw how he treated the people who worked for him, and I don't want any part of being a doormat for some overinflated ego."

"Joey Martin was and is a great quarterback, but he's also a crummy person and a lousy friend. I know this and you know this. I took his abuse professionally—you took it personally. But one bad relationship with an athlete should not make you pass up good business opportunities with another. Replacing Joey with Luke as a client was one of my best decisions ever. He's the top pitcher in the game of baseball, yet he's as down-to-earth as they come. Give him a chance, Katie."

"I have no trouble getting clients," Katie clarified for him, and it was the truth. She worked mainly on the road, doing security for the music industry, having once been a dancer for one of the *it* singers of the decade, until she blew out her knee. But with a cop for a father, she'd been drawn to security, and learned all the ins and outs. One day, she and her father had planned to open Lyons Security and cater to high-end clientele...only her father hadn't lived to see their dream fulfilled. He and her mother had died in a car accident three years before. While Carrie had been a senior in college.

"I'm proud of you and how well your business has done. But how many of those jobs pay what I have offered?"

Katie frowned. "Ron," she said with an apology in her voice. "I owe you for a lot of moral support in the past. I don't want you to think the money is the only reason I'm here."

He smiled, his expression softening. He had always been like a second father to her. It's why she had even told him about Carrie. If it had been anyone else, she would have kept it private.

"I don't think that," he reassured her. "But I do know you need the money, so it helped me get you here. Now, let's proceed with the introductions, shall we?"

"A file and a rundown on his security system would be nice."

"Tomorrow," he said. "It's late. You just got here. The introduction is the most important thing tonight."

Katie nodded and followed Ron into a large, dimly lit room with a full bar against one wall. She caught her first glimpse of Luke as he stood behind the bar.

And damn if her stomach didn't flip-flop. Even her mouth went dry. Her reaction was over-the-top, and not at all expected.

He was sexy as hell and exactly the kind of guy Katie had sworn off years before. With determination, she pushed her instant attraction to him out of her mind. One run-in with a professional athlete was enough to last a lifetime, thank you very much.

Even taller than she had pictured, he was a dominating

figure, towering well over the top of the bar. His broad, dark good looks were far more devastating to the female senses, at least hers, in person than they were on television or in magazines.

Ron, a black man who looked more like a linebacker than like Luke's manager, walked toward the bar, smiling at Luke as he did.

He positioned himself on a bar stool and motioned Katie forward. "Come meet Luke."

"Yes," Luke said in a voice that almost seemed to taunt. Then he added, "Come meet Luke."

Okay. That, most definitely, was a taunt.

At least his personality wasn't going to draw her the way his features did. "Don't have to," she mumbled to herself. "Met one arrogant athlete, met 'em all."

"What?" Ron asked.

Katie smiled at Ron, her lips tight, her muscles tense. "Nothing."

"Nothing she wants to repeat," Luke said, drawing her attention. Then he winked at her.

Katie frowned, still standing just inside the doorway, her feet seemingly cemented to the floor. For some reason she was reluctant to move forward, as if she were entering the lion's den. Had the lion himself heard her from clear across the room?

Surely not. Yet…the look on Luke's face said yes. Not that she cared. Let him hear. They needed to establish right up front that she wasn't a rug to be walked on.

When she spoke again, she made sure he heard her. "Smarter than the average athlete. Point for you."

He laughed. "Good. I like being on top."

Her eyes narrowed as she scrutinized him. Was there

a double meaning to his words? His eyebrow inched up as if he knew what she was thinking and dared her to say it out loud. Which made her wonder if her mind was that dirty, and she'd taken his words out of context…or was he trying to get her to second-guess herself?

"Luke is a lot of things, but average isn't one of them," Ron said to Katie, drawing her attention as he patted the bar stool. "Come join us."

Katie didn't look at Luke. Didn't have to. She could feel him gloating across the room. His attitude, even from a distance, was a prime example of why she didn't like working with athletes. They were all jerks.

Already she knew Luke Winter had an exceptional knack for pushing her buttons. No, she most definitely did not like working with athletes.

And no way was she going to be attracted to Luke Winter. So her body reacting like this made no sense. No way was she getting involved with another athlete. She would do this job and then be gone. Luke Winter could not get to her. It was impossible. Squaring her shoulders, a look of determination in her eyes, she stepped forward.

She advanced toward the offered seat. "Good," she said to Ron, and despite the fact that she was talking about Luke, she didn't look at him. "Average athletes don't know how to follow directions. I'll need Mr. Winter to do as I say."

Luke laughed. "Oh, now, darlin', I'm sure we can work something out. If you ask me just right, I'll do about anything."

That stopped her in her tracks. Slowly, her gaze moved to his. "Mr. Winter…"

"Luke," he corrected. "Call me Luke. I plan to call you Katie."

Katie kept her expression impassive.

But just barely.

She wasn't about to get sucked into whatever game this man was trying to play. She started forward again, even as she met Luke's piercing gaze. There was something intimate about the way he looked at her, his eyes lingering on her features in a slow, thorough inspection.

His scrutiny was keen and far too probing, as if he were seeing well below the surface. It set her on edge, made her feel off center. Each step forward came slowly and took extra effort.

With irritation, she realized she was holding her breath. She immediately forced herself to exhale, slowly allowing the air to trickle through her lips.

Ron was talking, and she tried to focus on what he was saying. Not quite at the bar, she drew to a halt, still struggling to absorb Luke's words.

"Katie and I go way back," Ron commented. "I trust her as a person, and her company is considered top-notch. She's provided security for some big names. People who tend to draw the type of problem you are having. This won't be her first stalker."

Katie's eyes flickered from Ron back to Luke as she settled her hands on the back of the bar stool. Their eyes locked and held, almost squaring off in silent battle.

"No," she said to Ron, but never took her gaze off Luke. "Is it your first, Mr. Winter?"

Thanks to Ron, Katie already knew Luke didn't take

seriously the recent threats he'd been receiving, and that he didn't want her or anyone else's help.

According to Ron, Luke was a very private person. Katie wasn't sure she bought into that idea. Especially since Ron had also said Luke was a nice guy. Clearly he was mistaken on that point, which meant he could be wrong on others. Luke reeked of arrogance and trouble. Not a hint of niceness.

Luke's full attention was on her. She could feel it with every ounce of her being. His lips twitched ever so slightly. "It depends on how you define *stalker.* I've had my share of obsessive fans."

In an effort not to look into his eyes, her gaze slipped down…to his lips. Another strategic mistake. They were full, the bottom bigger than the top, and alluring. Addictive…yes. She could see why a fan or two had become obsessive. He had a vibrant sensuality that demanded a reaction, even by her, despite her resistance.

No way was he a nice guy. He had bad boy, hot nights and great orgasms written all over him. Tempting, spicy, delicious, never nice.

Not that she cared.

She didn't need sex. Two years of going without had proven that. So why was she feeling all this damn awareness in every inch of her body, for a man she didn't even like?

One who didn't even want her here.

She forced her mind to business. "Obsessive enough to send death threats?"

Luke shrugged off the question. "The letters are harmless."

"They're getting more aggressive," Katie told him

sternly. "I saw them, and I don't like the way the tone has changed."

Luke's lips thinned. "A letter never killed anyone."

"But I might," Ron muttered. "Luke, get on board. There is more to this than letters. What about the hang-up calls on your private line?"

Luke made a frustrated sound. "You're making too much of this, Ron. I don't need extra security, and I don't have a stalker. I have a fan who is a bit over-the-top. That's all."

Katie didn't think Ron was overreacting. How would a fan get his private line? "I think Ron has reason to be concerned."

Luke narrowed his eyes on her. "And you're going to keep me snug and safe?"

His words held a hint of challenge. "From the stalker," she bit out, "but if you keep pushing me, I can't promise *I* won't hurt you."

His head fell back as he laughed. It was a deep, reso-nating sound that reached out and warmed her insides in a way that was sexy as hell and impossible to ignore. Damn him.

"That might be fun," he said with a twinkle in his eyes.

2

LUKE STARED at Katie Lyons from across the bar, and the corners of his mind flickered with a unique response. What it was, he wasn't quite sure, but damn if it wasn't impossible to ignore. His body felt alive with her presence. His heart was beating at a crazy fast pace, and ridiculously, Luke had to force away the urge to put a fist over it. Despite his resolve to dislike Katie, the distinct thunder of attraction jolted his nerve endings.

Somehow, getting her to hate him now seemed far from appealing. But it was too late to turn back. Besides, the last damn thing he needed was a woman to screw him over with her own private agenda. He had no intention of expanding his emotional stamina, though as she smiled, sexy, all pride and defiance, he thought his physical stamina might be worth testing. Damn, he wanted her, and he cursed the irony of finding no one tempting for months, until this woman—the one he was trying to shake loose. Katie was hands-off. Yeah, right. Tell that to his cock. He was rock hard, his zipper stretched, his balls drawn up tight in discomfort.

"Drink?" Luke asked, watching her climb up on a bar

stool as he tried to decide what his next action should be. What was it about this woman that did funny things to his insides?

Turned him on.

Beyond that even...

Interested him. No, that still wasn't a strong enough word. Intrigued him was more like it. When was the last time a woman had gotten his attention the way this one did? He couldn't remember. At some point they had all become users to him. The thought was so cynical, and so out of character, he made a mental note to revisit exactly what was going on in his head.

Katie's voice, a sultry sound that wrapped around him like an enticing breeze on a hot day, drew him back into the present. "No, thank you," she said with obviously forced politeness, which did nothing to douse the sexiness of her tone or the way it rippled along his nerve endings.

Despite the businesslike mask she wore, he could see a softer, and even hotter, Katie beneath. Her eyes were a warm green, like grass, with little specks of yellow. Her brown hair hung down her shoulders in soft waves, and he could just imagine burying his hands in it while he kissed her.

He could tell from the way she shifted slightly that she knew how intense his scrutiny was. She continued, "I'd like to get straight to the point. You have real trouble here."

Luke leaned an elbow on the bar. "Ron is the one who thinks I have trouble. I don't. As I have already stated, we are simply dealing with a fan who is a bit more aggressive than others."

Katie quirked an eyebrow as she leaned forward and rested one palm on the bar. "Then what am I doing here?"

Luke's eyes flicked to Ron. "Making *him* happy."

Katie pushed off the bar as if preparing to leave. "Then I don't see any point in staying. Unless I have your buy-in, Mr. Winter, my services are useless."

Ron responded immediately. "Luke will cooperate fully. His coach wants this."

That got Luke's attention. "Since when?"

Ron's voice had a hard edge. "Since the team's water supply was tampered with."

"When did this happen?" Katie asked immediately.

Luke spoke to Ron, ignoring her question. "That was a prank and you damn well know it," he said hotly. "Salt. It was flipping salt."

Ron's expression was one of frustration. "It was a sign we need to be more cautious. Think of the rest of your team, Luke. This is serious business."

"This is crazy, is what it is!" Luke said as he stiffened his spine. "A load of crap if ever I've heard one."

Ron stood up. "You've had a great preseason, Luke. You're good—you're damn good—and you'd be a loss to the team. But both management and the league feel there've been too many incidents to let you go into the regular season without extra security. They won't risk the liability of endangering players, fans and staff."

Luke scoffed. "This isn't about me, Ron, and we both know it. It's about the guy who beat up an umpire last season, and the fight that broke out in the stands and the two players who got killed. Management is worried about liability over things I had nothing to do with."

"If you weren't being targeted," Ron argued, "you wouldn't be a focal point. And it's neither here nor there because bottom-lining it here, Luke, without proper precautions, your season is over before it starts. And Katie has the credentials to make management confident we've taken those precautions."

Tension climbed a path up Luke's spine. Everything was going wrong. He didn't need this right now. Not when he was trying to stay focused on his game, and come back from scandal with a strong season. Inhaling, he tried to calm himself, to think logically. Then, unintentionally, Luke's gaze collided with Katie's. To his surprise, her eyes softened, seemed to reflect understanding.

He liked her, he thought. Damn it to hell, he liked her. He didn't want to, but he did. Instinctively trusted her even, and based on his recent judgments, that should be enough to send him running to the hills. He'd learned the hard way with past relationships about how dangerous trust could be.

People wanted things from him. They didn't just want to be his friend. Not without a reason.

"I know this is difficult, Mr. Winter," she said in a gentle, almost comforting voice, as if she actually cared how he felt.

She still wouldn't call him by his first name and for some reason that really set him off. "Luke. My name is Luke." The woman was driving him insane, and he had known her mere minutes. The last thing he wanted was for her to get close enough to know what really got to him—he needed her gone. Lashing back at her incredible ability to get under his skin, trying to upset

her, Luke gave her a quick, intimate, up-and-down perusal meant to stir her anger. It was a look that held an
intentionally blatant message—*you'd be a great piece
of ass*. Of course he would never confirm that assessment. She didn't like him, nor did he want her to like
him. He'd chosen a plan and he was sticking to it—she
had to hate him.

KATIE CAST Ron a pleading look, silently asking for
guidance. In reply, Ron quietly repeated, "He'll be
reasonable."

But in the flash of a second that Katie had looked
away from Luke, he'd advanced on her, and she had a
feeling it wasn't because he intended to "behave." Suddenly, he was standing beside her, the spicy male scent
of arrogant, pain-in-the-backside man, invading her
nostrils and her space. Trying to regain the composure
she rarely lost but that Luke was managing to rattle,
Katie remained facing the bar, both palms flattened on
the wooden surface. Tilting her chin to the side, she cut
him a suspicious look—wondering what he was up to,
and he *was* up to something, of that she was certain.

Covertly, she took in his appearance—she simply
couldn't help herself. It was her first time to see his
entire body. And what a body it was. He was dressed
casually in snug-fitting jeans and an equally snug black
tee, both of which molded ever so nicely to the rippling
length of his powerful body. Physically the man was
nothing shy of outright impressive. Even his foul mood
didn't take away from the pure maleness of his presence,
and the perfection of his athletic body.

With a facade of control that defied her racing heart

and the funny fluttery thing in her stomach, Katie dared to give Ron her back as she turned to face her challenger. It was unsettling that she wasn't as capable of dismissing Luke Winter as she was the rest of the bigger-than-Texas egos she'd encountered in the wild world of professional sports.

She and Luke now stood face-to-face, each with an elbow propped on the bar, neither blinking, a standoff of sorts, one she feared she was losing. His nearness washed over her in a wave of warm, tingling sensations that tested her cool exterior and threatened her mask of aloofness. She was certain she was the one who would break, when something unexpected happened. For an instant, a tiny instant, the arrogance of the big, bad baseball pitcher melted into vulnerability. Taken off guard, Katie blinked and it was gone, replaced by something much different, more tense, almost angry.

He laughed, but there wasn't any hint of humor in the deeply resonating sound. "I don't see how you are going to stop anyone from hurting me." Again he was taunting, and Katie couldn't help but wonder if he was punishing her for seeing something in him that he hadn't wanted exposed. He continued his verbal assault, "I believe a large woman could overpower you. A man would easily control you."

His eyes made a slow, lazy tour down her body and then back up again, blatantly pausing at her breasts. When his eyes met hers again, she wanted to reach over and smack his face. The hand that hung by her side balled into a fist as she willed herself to calm, glaring at him with what she hoped was fire. Not once now, but twice, he had taken the liberty of undressing her with his eyes.

"Ron," he said in a slow drawl, his eyes remaining on Katie. "Really, now. Let's be realistic here. She looks more like one of my groupies than a security expert." His lips twisted. "Then again, she is a beauty. She might be entertaining."

Ron grunted. Loudly. "You're out of line, Luke. Enough. You are not only insulting Katie, you're underestimating her." Suddenly, Katie was aware of Ron standing to her left, but she didn't dare take her eyes off Luke. They remained facing each other, glaring at each other. Katie felt Ron's attention land heavily on Luke. "You really are being difficult, my man. What's come over you?"

"I don't know what you mean, Ron." Luke never took his eyes off Katie. "Why don't we see what she really can do?"

Suddenly, Katie found herself trapped, her back against the bar, imprisoned by one of Luke's strong arms on either side of her.

"Luke!" Ron's angry voice rumbled as if in a tunnel.

Unwilling to be manhandled, Katie considered pulling the gun in her boot and teaching Luke a real lesson but thought better of it. Instead, she pressed her hands to that warm, hard chest and raised a knee, stopping the instant before she made contact. To her satisfaction, Luke's eyes went wide with the near impact.

"The way to satisfy a man might not always be in his pants," she said, slowly easing her leg down, her hand staying on that hard wall of muscle, keeping him at a distance. "But right now, it darn sure is mine."

"So you like to play dirty, do you?" His breath teased as it trickled along her cheek.

His fast, unaffected comment drew a glare from Katie. "You, Luke Winter," she muttered between her teeth, trying not to think about the way his thighs were suddenly pressed to hers, "are *way* too full of your-self." And his lips were way too close, as well. Sensual lips. Full lips. She snapped her attention away from his mouth, irritated at her distraction. "I'm not a groupie or even a fan. Frankly, I think you pitchers ruin the game. It's boring. Nobody hits the ball."

"Wait. You think baseball is boring?"

She smiled even before she got the words out. "Just pitchers." Her hands slid from his chest and she crossed her arms in front of her, silently dismissing him.

"But you think I'm a good pitcher."

She blinked at the odd comment. "I didn't say that."

"I think you did."

She almost threw her hands in the air. "The point is—I don't care about your pitching. I've dated my pro athlete."

"Who?"

"Joey Martin."

"The quarterback?"

"Yes."

"Ah. I know Joey. Arrogant guy. It's a quarterback thing. Pitchers are better. But I can see why you're bitter."

Exasperated, she exclaimed, "I am *not* bitter. And

back to my point that I never quite made. I've dated my athlete. Got the T-shirt and don't want another. You have nothing I want or need." Ron groaned in frustration, though neither Luke nor Katie paid him any mind.

With a sizzling, heavy-lidded stare, Luke leaned in close. "You keep telling yourself that, sweetheart, and maybe you'll believe it." A shiver raced down her spine at the intense look that followed. "In my experience, people scream the loudest about the very things they are running from."

She laughed in disbelief at the implication. "You think I'm running from *you?*"

His damnable silver-gray eyes overflowed with challenge. "Aren't you?"

"If anyone is running," she countered, poking his chest, "it's you."

His gaze dropped to his chest where she'd touched him and so did hers. Something happened in that split second. Tension entwined with attraction and exploded. Heat pooled low in her belly, awareness charging a path along her limbs, tightening her nipples, heart pounding in her ears. Slowly, their eyes lifted at the same instant, colliding in an electric charge of pure, red-hot attraction. It was one of those moments, one of those liquid fire moments between a man and a woman, that could turn animosity into wild, passionate sex.

"That's enough!" Ron's voice snapped through the air, and Katie all but jumped at the reminder of why she couldn't have passionate anything with Luke. He was a job, a duty, a pain-in-the-backside, arrogant jerk. But still neither she nor Luke moved. They just kept staring at each other.

Ron's hands closed down on one of each of their arms. "I *said*—that's enough."

Luke backed away, a smile tilting his way-too-hot mouth upward—the mouth Katie couldn't stop staring at, wondering what it would feel like pressed to hers. Oh, God, she was thinking about kissing Luke Winter. Was she insane? Shaken to the core, she jerked her attention from Luke's face, ran her hand along the edge of her hair and made her decision.

"Obviously, this isn't going to work." A second later, she was making fast tracks toward the door. She'd been crazy to come here, and she knew it. Ron should have known, too.

Luke's voice mocked her from behind. "She gives up easily," he said, evidently talking to Ron. "Why exactly did you recommend her? You thought she might actually have some balls? Guess you were wrong."

Katie abruptly turned around, anger flashing in her brown eyes. "I cannot work effectively when it's clear I will not have your cooperation. We can't work together. We can't even have a conversation together."

Luke laughed loudly, leaving a trail of arrogant satisfaction ringing in the air. "Like I said, you give up easily."

Katie fought for composure, enduring his mocking laughter with an internal cringe.

"Katie," Ron said, his own exasperation apparent in the tension-etched way he said her name. "I don't know what the hell has come over Luke, but we need you. He needs you. I need you. The entire team needs you." He gave Luke a biting look. "Luke *will* behave himself. I'll make sure of it." He returned his attention to Katie.

"Take the job." With a pointed meaning, he added, "We both know you need it."

Luke's eyebrows arched sharply. Katie, in turn, shot Ron an angry look of reproach. Her financial picture was none of Luke Winter's business, and that was exactly where this was leading.

Ron ignored her silent reprimand and spoke to Luke. "Management wants this to happen. I suggest you make it work."

Then he waved his hand between the two of them, pointing at each. "So, to both of you, listen carefully to what I have to say. Katie, you need this job. Luke, you can take Katie or be left behind. There are plenty of young bucks dying to get your starting spot in the lineup. You might think you aren't replaceable, but so has every other pitcher who's ever been replaced. Both of you decide now. Are we going to make this work or not?"

Katie and Luke stared at each other, neither in a happy mood. Neither gloating any longer.

Ron continued, "I take that as acceptance from both of you. Now," he said, crossing his arms in front of his brawny chest, "we need to sort out the logistics. No one can know who Katie really is." Ron turned to Katie. "Luke is single, and so are you. I say you go undercover as his girlfriend."

Her rejection was instant. "Forget it," she spat at Ron. "That's a deal breaker. I'm *not* going to pretend to be this man's girlfriend!" She narrowed her gaze, accusation in her voice. "You planned this from the beginning. I know you, Ron. You knew I wouldn't agree to this kind of setup, so you waited until I was here. That is low. I expected more from you."

"Management wants this problem to appear to disappear," Ron explained. "That means they want Luke's extra security to be invisible. And let's face it, our stalker doesn't need to be alerted that someone is watching or that person might pull back before we catch them. This plan solves all of these issues." Ron set his jaw, unaffected by her words, apparently prepared for them. "I'll throw in an extra five thousand a week. That should cover any discomfort."

Katie opened her mouth to reject the offer, indignant about Ron's behavior, but forced herself to shut it again. She needed the money to get her sister out of trouble, but damn it, she didn't want to be bought.

Then, suddenly, she realized Luke hadn't said a word. Not one objection, not one complaint, nothing. She looked at him, a question in her mind that was most assuredly on her face.

Why wasn't he complaining? Why was he leaning lazily against the bar, one long leg crossed in front of the other. "Why aren't you objecting?" she asked suspiciously.

He shrugged a broad shoulder. "I want to play ball, thus I accept my circumstances. Seems you're the one who still has issues."

"I have issues?" she asked in disbelief. How had this gotten turned around to her? She turned businesslike, her voice softer now by design. "I just don't think this is the best approach."

"I'm open to hearing a better one," Ron said, leaning on the bar beside Luke. "You got one?"

Katie swallowed. Ron's idea was a good one. She just didn't like it. "Well, no, not yet."

"So this is our best option for now?" Ron asked, with an expectant look on his face.

Damn. She was trapped. If her sister didn't have this gambling debt, she'd refuse altogether. But what option did she have? Carrie had sharks after her. "I, um, suppose so."

Luke challenged her then. "Then what's the problem?"

LUKE HAD already figured out it was not in Katie's nature to walk away from a challenge, exactly why he'd pushed her, egging her on. And for some unknown, crazy reason, the thought of her leaving kicked his ass. His plan to scare her off had only served to make him want her more.

And when she'd pulled that knee on him…the fire in her eyes, well…it had sent heat straight through his veins and right to the vicinity of her target.

It was like a white-hot rocket had settled between his thighs. He had stood before her, completely hard and wanting. Katie Lyons might be a problem, but she was a delicious one.

So now he found himself baiting her, and she was letting him. "Is there a problem, Katie?"

He watched her force a smile. And damn if she wasn't cute as hell trying to act all tough when he could tell she really wanted to bolt. Sexy and cute? Had he ever found a woman he would call both?

Even as he was acting on his attraction to her, and challenging her to stay around, in the far corners of his mind he knew he was setting himself up to get burned again. But he couldn't seem to help himself. He wanted to find out what made Katie tick. What made her laugh? What made her sigh?

Several tension-filled seconds passed where he could almost see her trying to form words, before she finally managed to actually do so. "No problem," she finally said. "We'll do it Ron's way." It was a weak concession, at best, but one Luke reveled in nonetheless.

Ron smiled his approval. "Good. It's settled, then." He glanced at Luke. "Katie will go undercover as your girlfriend. We have a week before you leave for the first series. That'll give her time to get her crew here and in place." Ron looked at Katie. "Luke has plenty of room for you to stay here."

Katie had opened her mouth to voice what Luke was certain would be an objection, when Ron turned to Luke. "Katie is known for solving problems fast. She gets up close and personal with the client and smokes out the problem, like fire in a chimney. It's amazing."

Luke studied Ron, and then let his focus shift back to Katie. "Is that so?" To Luke's surprise, she started blushing, and he found himself gently adding, "Good thing I have a guest bedroom next door to mine."

She wet her lips, choosing to divert the conversation away from the bedroom next to his. "I have two of my staff members joining us tomorrow. We'll have to discuss their cover stories rather quickly after they arrive." She paused. "They'll need rooms, as well."

Luke inclined his head, forcing himself not to smile at her, diverting the conversation away from their sleeping arrangements. She had just agreed to stay around.

And for some unidentifiable reason, he felt the best he had in months.

"Not a problem," Luke told her. "Why don't I show you to your room?"

She bit her bottom lip. "I know it's late, but I'd like to go down a list of questions with you tonight so I can start formulating a plan of attack." She glanced at Ron. "I'm empty-handed. I have no file. No real data to work with."

"I'll bring it by tomorrow," Ron promised.

Luke wanted nothing more than to start getting to know Katie tonight, but she looked tired and more than a little uncomfortable, despite her grand efforts to appear unscathed. "Your flight was late," he said. "And the trip from New York to Los Angeles is a long one. Why don't we start bright and early in the morning?"

"I'd…" She seemed to reconsider what she was going to say. "That works."

He smiled at her, a sincere, heartfelt smile. Now that she'd agreed to take the case, he needed to stop with the games. It was time to show her he wasn't such a bad guy.

"I'll carry your bags up for you." Luke faced Ron. "I'd like to talk to you before you leave."

"If you have something to say about me, say it to my face."

Katie's heated words drew his attention. He narrowed his gaze on her—his intention had been to question Ron about Katie. But maybe that was best done directly.

"Then let's make a deal," Luke said to her.

Her eyes darkened. "What kind of deal?"

Ron answered before Luke could. "You two deal,"

he said. "I need to get going anyway. Unlike the two of you, age isn't on my side. It's eleven o'clock, and I have a meeting at seven in the morning."

"I'll walk out with you," Katie said quickly.

Luke laughed.

Katie fixed him in a hard stare. "What?" she demanded.

He shook his finger at her. "You don't play by the rules."

"What does that mean?" she asked, but her expression said she knew.

"I'm out of here," Ron said, moving toward the door. "And for the record," he called over his shoulder, turning back to them for a quick moment, "I won't be the referee. Play nice together and catch a bad guy. Then we all win."

He opened the door and disappeared.

Luke and Katie were suddenly alone, staring at each other, the air crackling with awareness. Ah, but Luke was not blind. There was a heavy dose of discomfort on Katie's part, as well. She wanted him, but she didn't want to want him. Whatever Joey Martin had done to her, he'd done it well.

Okay, admittedly, Luke playing the asshole on deck hadn't helped. He'd taken a preexisting wall and inched it higher. Which really sucked because he liked her. She was real. He sensed it as surely as he did a batter about to hike a ball out of the park, sensed this with such certainty that he wouldn't bother second-guessing himself, even though his recent track record with women was pretty flipping pathetic. If Katie hated him, it would be openly, not behind his back. If she desired him, her passion would be bold and flaming hot.

"So, Katie Lyons," he said softly as he took a step toward her. "Let's make that deal I mentioned."

Her eyes went wide, suspicion flickering in their depths. "What kind of deal?"

"The way I see it," he said as he closed the distance between them, "we have two options for dealing with our situation."

She swallowed and then tilted her chin up defiantly. "Okay, I'll bite. What two options are those?"

He took another step. She didn't move. She stood her ground with that tough facade, but he knew she was wavering by the flash of nervousness in her eyes.

"We could fight all day and all night," he said. He stopped in front of her, close. So close all he had to do was lift his arms to touch her. Damn, he loved her scent, a soft floral something. He wasn't much of a flower guy, but he thought maybe honeysuckle. Sweet. A contradiction from her tough exterior, a detail that ripened his assessment of her to downright delicious.

"Or?" she prodded, refusing to back away. Damn, she had spunk. That made him hot.

"Or we can get right to the root of the problem and be done with it." He shifted closer to her, his lips lingering above hers. "Now would be a good time for that knee if you don't want to be kissed." He reached for her, pulling her close, molding her sexy, taut body to his. He didn't give her time to object. His mouth closed down on hers.

He kissed her, prodding her into a response. She started to resist, her palms pressed against his chest, her spine stiff. But when his tongue dipped into her mouth and brushed hers, she whimpered. Her lips softened, her body warmed. She melted and gave him what he really wanted.

Her surrender.

3

KATIE COULD NOT stop kissing Luke Winter. The man deserved that well-placed knee for daring to kiss her, on top of being a complete, utter ass. And she'd give him that knee. Soon. Very soon. Right after she finished kissing him. And, oh, God, was she kissing him. The kind of kissing that screamed *Strip me naked and have your way with me*. Worse, no matter how hard she willed herself to pull away from such abandon, Katie couldn't do it. She was drowning in sexy male seduction and couldn't find the desire to escape. Which led her to one conclusion—Luke Winter had a magic tongue. It was the only explanation for the drugging effect of his kiss, the only explanation for the dull, wonderful ache that spread through her limbs and coiled in her stomach. When was the last time a man had accomplished such a feat? A year? Almost two?

So when he said, "Tell me this feels as good to you as it does to me," with his lips lingering above hers, a whisper from another caress, Katie tried to say no, but she was afraid he would stop kissing her.

Instead, she whispered, "Yes." And it was breathless. Hungry.

Bingo. He kissed her again.

She knew she should be pushing him away, but...he tasted and felt so darn good. She was human after all, and he was...well, he was a damn good kisser.

And try as she might to ignore the reaction her body was having to him, she couldn't. She wanted him.

Bad.

But this was just a kiss. No harm, no foul. At least, in her desire-stricken state, that was the logic she decided to cling to. Later she would chastise herself.

Not now.

Besides, it had been an eternity, or so it seemed, since she had been thoroughly kissed. His tongue played along the sides of hers, and Katie moaned without any possible hope of restraining the sound.

There was something so warm, so alluringly perfect about his kisses. Perhaps the way he used his lips to caress hers, or maybe it was the way his tongue did this slow, seductive dance along hers.

Or was there more?

Some kind of unique chemistry between them perhaps?

Slowly, he pulled away from her, coming back for a brief nibble, before staring down at her with a probing, heated gaze.

Without thought, a sigh of pure female satisfaction slipped from her mouth.

He smiled in return—clearly proud of making her act in such a way—but Katie didn't find the smile offensive, surprisingly. She knew he had enjoyed kissing her, as well.

His hand slid beneath her hair, his callused fingers caressing her neck with delicious friction. "Katie—"

Someone cleared their throat at the doorway, a distinctly feminine sound, drawing their attention. Shocked at someone else's presence, Katie instantly moved to take a step backward. Luke quickly settled his hands around her waist, holding her there against him. Katie cast him a disbelieving look and had opened her mouth to complain when he whispered, "Remember your cover. We're dating."

"I think we're about to have our first fight," she ground out, giving him her best evil glare, intended for perps under arrest but quite effective with low-life athletes who couldn't keep it in their pants. Her attention shifted to the visitor, a woman—no, girl—not more than nineteen. Distress etched her youthful features, a frown on her heart-shaped face. Her faded, ripped jeans and pretty yellow lace blouse were as youthful as the highlights streaking her long, dark hair. A sick feeling gathered in Katie's stomach. Apparently, Luke Winter liked them young, and he didn't care if he had more than one woman in his house at once. She visualized the pleasure she'd get from a well-placed knee, something she should have already given him. Pig!

"Hi, Jessica," Luke said. "Katie, this—"

Jessica rambled over the top of him. "I should have known better than to let myself—" Her hands twisted together, her voice trailing off.

"Let yourself what?" Luke said, actually having the gall to sound both concerned and confused.

Katie would have told him where to stick that stupid act of his, too, but the girl spoke up first. "My mother wanted me to let you know the guest room is ready." Her hate-filled gaze shifted to Katie. "She said you'd need it."

Katie blinked and turned to Luke. "Who's her mother?" What the heck did the man have going on here?

"I am," came a voice etched with accent. A gentle-looking older woman stepped up beside Jessica, her thick, dark hair streaked with gray and pinned in a bun. "I'm Maria Rodriguez, Luke's housekeeper." She paused and smiled at Luke. "But he's more like a son to me." Her friendly attention, so unlike her daughter's, shifted to Katie. "You must be the someone special Ron told me Luke had arriving this evening. We let ourselves in. To make sure you had everything you needed."

"Someone special?" Katie repeated. She swallowed, biting back anger—and not at Luke this time. She and Ron were going to have words. He had clearly planned the dating thing from the start and thrown her to the wolves—no plan, no story in the mix. And now she and Luke were flying by the seat of their pants. Lacing her arm with Luke's, she forced a smile in his direction. "Is that what I'm being called these days? Should I tell you what my special name for you is?"

Luke slid his hand over hers. "Why don't we save that for when we're alone, sweetheart." He pulled her a bit closer, their hips aligned, and the message clear— he was more than happy to play boyfriend. No doubt because he thought he was going to be getting more of that kiss-kiss action.

They'd be clearing up that misconception sooner rather than later. It was time to recover from this unexpected meeting and get her ducks in a row. This was business, not pleasure, which she should never have forgotten.

Speaking to Maria, Luke added, "The 'someone special' comment is Ron's way of being discreet about Katie and I dating. You know how I dislike the media delving into my personal life."

"Hound dogs, those reporters," Maria said with a huff. "I get sick of them snooping around, and I'm not the one they are trying to snap photos of." She pursed her lips toward Katie. "Hope they don't run you off."

"If anyone runs me off," Katie said, squeezing Luke's arm meaningfully, "I can assure you, it will be Luke." She glanced at him, their eyes clashing in a strained connection before she forced a smile in Maria's direction. "And it's nice to meet you, by the way."

Katie's attention flickered to Jessica, whom she'd concluded either a) had a big-time crush on Luke, or b) was sleeping with him, or maybe even c) had slept with him at one point and hoped to again. Whatever the case, she was going on the suspect list. "Nice to meet you, as well, Jessica."

Jessica gave her a barely there nod and then eyed Luke, speaking to him, not Katie. "She's in the room next to yours." There was a message there—*I know she isn't sleeping with you.*

Maria quickly responded, as if she sensed her daughter's agitation and inference, and was trying to cover it up. "It's a beautiful room," she said. "Let me know if I can do anything for you while you're here, Katie."

Jessica remained focused on Luke. "Should I show her to her room?"

Katie grimaced, disliking the way Jessica spoke as if she was not there.

A slow, intimate smile slipped onto Luke's lips as he glanced down at her. "I'll show Katie to her room myself." Okay. So if Jessica thought the separate rooms meant they were not sleeping together, Luke's stare, at that moment, must have rattled her. Because even Katie was almost convinced she was sleeping with Luke based on that hot, steamy look.

Maria cleared her throat, her cheeks red. "We'll leave you for the night and head home. Oh, and Katie, your bag is in your room."

"Thank you," Kate said quickly. At the same moment, Luke slid his arm back over Katie's shoulder, another intimate, overly friendly gesture. She wanted to shove him away, especially when little ripples of awareness began spraying along her nerve endings. She had so many reasons to dislike this man, yet her body couldn't seem to get in agreement with that rationale. Nor did she have time to dart away when Maria and Jessica finally departed.

The instant she and Luke were alone, Luke turned to face her, pulling her to him, hands still around her waist. "You thought Jessica and I were together."

Denial seemed futile. "Are you?" she challenged, her fingers melded to those damn, far-too-appealing muscular arms.

"She's my housekeeper's daughter, Katie," he said, his voice laced with disbelief. "I was at her sweet-sixteen party. She's a kid. I have not, nor would I ever, sleep with Jessica. You really want to hate me, don't you?"

Yes! And it would be easier if he would let her go and stop touching her. "You've not exactly given me reason to do anything but hate you."

She got her wish. He dropped his hands from her waist and stared at her. "Because I was trying to get rid of you, and for the record, I know I was a jerk and I'm sorry. But you have to admit you were an easy target, with all kinds of preconceived notions about me."

Her eyes went wide. "You admit you were a jerk?"

"Yes," he said pointedly, hands on his hips. "And I said I'm sorry, in case you missed that part. Now it's your turn. Do you admit you judged me before meeting me?"

She sighed, crossing her arms in front of her chest, her foot tapping with nervous energy. It was true, she had prejudged him. "Okay, yes, I did, but I'm not apologizing. You were a jerk. I have no reason to believe it was an act."

"Do you make a habit of kissing jerks?"

"Apparently, I do," she replied shortly.

His expression darkened, eyes flashed. "I'm not him, you know."

She knew who he meant. Her ex. The one who had said he was different from all the others but wasn't. She chose to play dumb. "Who might that be?"

He nodded decisively. "Got it. You don't want to talk about the past, and that appears to be the root of all my evil."

"You learn fast," she said. "But you seem to create

your own evil quite nicely. You don't need anyone from my past to do it for you."

His jaw tensed, heat firing from his eyes, a mixture of anger and arousal. He wanted to kiss her into submission—she could see it in his eyes, and she barely contained the urge to back away.

"I'll drop it." Then he added with emphasis, "For now." He considered her a moment. "I'll show you to your room."

"Oh, no," Katie said with a nervous laugh. "I don't need you to escort me to my bedroom." She'd kissed him. She didn't want to do something crazy, like undress him, and considering she kept thinking about it, a solo trip to her room seemed smarter. "Just point me in the right direction."

His anger slid away with the appearance of a twinkle in his eyes. "Tucking tail and running?"

Yeah, she was, but she wasn't admitting that. She *was* running, and doing so fast and hard. Ripping his clothes off would get her nowhere but in trouble, yet she wanted to. Oh, boy, did she want to. That she was even thinking about it spoke volumes about where her head was right now, and it wasn't a place that allowed her to do her job. Luke was in danger. She was here to protect him, not get naked with him. It was time to get it together.

And yet, with that grand plan in mind, she still responded to his challenge, still could not resist saying, "I do not tuck tail and hide."

"I said run, not hide."

She shrugged. "Same thing."

"If you say so," he said, obviously unconvinced, but

he didn't push. "I'm hungry. You like Chinese food? There's a spot up the road that delivers."

She shook her head, trying to clear the skid marks from the sudden change of topic. "What game are you playing, Luke Winter?"

"No game. I'm hungry. I figured you might be, too."

He was trying to get her to let down her guard again. She wasn't a fool. This man and this situation were turning her upside down. "You're my client."

"Right," he said, reaching for a cordless phone on the bar and sitting down. "And that means what exactly?"

Her chin inched up. She wanted the parameters set. The line drawn in the sand. Directness seemed her best option. "I can't do this, Luke," she said.

"Eat with me or sleep with me?"

"I can't sleep with you."

He arched that damnably sexy eyebrow and said, "Chinese food is okay, though, right?"

She inhaled, suddenly feeling really not so good about her directness—embarrassed, in fact. Maybe he'd already played his game and won the kiss. Maybe he'd moved on, and she was making something big out of nothing. He was a jerk, and she'd become some passing notch on his belt.

"I'm not hungry, after all," she said. "I'd really prefer that you direct me to my room, and we can try starting fresh in the morning."

"Tell me," he said, resting his elbows on the bar, his dark tee stretching over well-honed muscle. "How are you going to play the role of my girlfriend when you're running away from me?"

Damn the man. "I'm not running."

"Prove it," he dared with a gleam in his eye that told her she should keep her mouth shut. "Stay here and eat with me."

"We'll have plenty of time to eat together on the road," she said. "And I have nothing to prove. I simply want to get some rest."

He considered her a moment. "First door on the right at the top of the stairs."

That was all she had to hear. Katie turned in flight, rushing toward the door, ready for escape. Running. Oh, yeah, she was running.

"Katie."

Something in his tone, in the softly spoken word, drew her to a pause at the door. She half turned, ready to complete her escape. "Yes?"

"I'm going to try to change your mind," he said. He wasn't talking about Chinese food. He was talking about sex.

"Don't," she said. "Don't try." But as she stepped into the hall, departing before he could say more, she knew she wanted him to try. Because *she* wanted *him*. She couldn't run. She couldn't hide. Not when she was sleeping in the man's house.

4

IT WAS almost midnight, a good forty-five minutes after Katie left Luke in his den. She'd showered in the private bathroom attached to her bedroom and changed into shorts and a T-shirt, her stomach growling with the absence of that Chinese food.

Katie sat cross-legged on top of a massive sleigh bed that was draped in a fluffy, navy-blue comforter, talking with her best friend and outrageously outspoken business partner, Donna Montgomery.

"Sleeping with Luke Winter could be the best thing you ever did," Donna said in the normal brazen fashion with which she approached life that somehow fit her fiery red hair and curves galore. "And since you're play dating him, you might as well get the benefits."

Leaning back against the array of throw pillows and pulling her knees to her chest, Katie rolled her eyes and embraced the levelheaded control she considered critical to her success, despite having shown none of it with Luke thus far. "That's insane. *You're* insane. No. Sleeping with Luke Winter would be insane."

"Some people would say *not* sleeping with a man

like that would be insane," Donna insisted. "I'm one of those people, by the way."

"Really?" Katie said in mock disbelief. "I would never have guessed that."

"You know what they say," she added. "If you fall off a bike, get back on and ride again. Ride another athlete, sweetheart. Then maybe you can finally move on from Joey."

"Oh, good grief," Katie said. "I do not need an athlete to *ride*. I moved past Joey Martin a long time ago. I never loved that man to start with."

"Oh, I know that," she said. "Joey's power over you had nothing to do with Joey. It was about your knee being blown out and your dancing career with it. But it left you guarded. You have to move on, not from Joey, but from yourself." She hesitated and then softened her voice. "It's been years, Katie. Do what you need to do to put the past to rest, but put it to rest."

"It's resting," she said. "I've simply been too busy to date. If the right guy comes around, I will. But Luke Winter isn't that guy. He's a client." Which was why the molten attraction to him could go nowhere.

"You mean he's a ballplayer," Donna said.

"That's irrelevant," Katie reminded her.

"Actually it's quite relevant," Donna countered. "It's a chance to be empowered. Have a hot fling and move on, and do so with a smile on your face. As Nike says— Just do it! Besides, you said he doesn't take these threats seriously. Sometimes the woman in a man's bed has the most influence on him."

Or the least, Katie thought drily. Which might be exactly what Luke hoped for. Sex with Luke might not keep her from doing her job, but it would keep him from taking her seriously. And sex complicating her relationship with Luke might well send her packing, and her sister was too important to risk this job going wrong.

"Luke is the one paying our salaries right now," Katie said. "Seriously, woman, where is your professionalism?"

"Oh, all right," Donna reluctantly acknowledged. "I guess you have a point."

"Finally," Katie announced. "Which brings us to the reason I took this job in the first place. How is my sister?"

"Carrie is a royal pain in the backside, as always, but she's safe. The girl couldn't find good sense if it was chasing her. How you two are related, I'll never understand. Are you sure your mom didn't cheat on your dad, and she's the product of an affair?"

"You ask me that all the time, so I'll ignore the question and move on."

"You always do, and I never get my answer. Funny that. Makes me wonder more." Then, as if Donna read her mind, which she often did, she added, "I delivered the first payment to those damn, bloodsucking sharks. Sorry bastards."

Katie laughed, embracing her friend's boisterous, opinionated and impossible-to-ignore personality to lighten the dark situation. Thank God for her.

"What?" Donna asked innocently—there was nothing innocent about Donna.

"Just loving that loud mouth of yours right about now," Katie admitted. "Get some sleep, woman." Katie sighed, but then remembered something. "Oh, wait. What time—"

"Ten o'clock on American Flight 202, but not until Saturday. They had a few bumps wrapping up their present assignment." And today was Wednesday. Damn. "They" referred to Noah and Josh, Katie's two most trusted security experts.

"What kind of bumps?" She pressed two fingers to the bridge of her nose. "Never mind. I don't want to know." She knew that they knew what they were doing. If they needed more time, they needed more time. She simply wanted company guarding Luke so she wasn't alone with him. "Just tell them to try and get here sooner. Thanks for always being on top of things, Donna," Katie said appreciatively. "Oh, and FYI, I should have a full file on Luke, and the threats he's received, early tomorrow. At least, that's what Ron promised me at the airport."

"I certainly would hope so," Donna said. "He rushed you to take this job as it is. If it's urgent so is the data for us to do our jobs."

"Agreed," Katie said. "But right now, we should both get some rest."

"Night-night, Katie dear. Dream sweet. May I suggest a theme? How about a little true undercover action with a certain sexy baseball player? A pitcher maybe?"

Katie laughed despite herself. "The only way you could know he's sexy is if you did an online search. And you did, didn't you?"

Donna snorted. "I watch television."

"You hate sports."

"But not the players," she said. "I'd love some baseball

player in nice tight pants. Oh, yes. I keep up with the highlights. Luke's a hottie. Admit it."

"Professionalism, Donna," Katie said, pretending ample indignation. "I'm hanging up."

"Meaning you think he's sexy."

"Hanging up *now,* Donna." And she did. Katie hit the end button on the phone and tossed it to the bed. The phone immediately rang again. She rolled her eyes and answered. "Donna. Good night already."

Silence.

"Donna?"

A strange feeling inched its way up her spine. This wasn't Donna or anyone else she called a friend. The line was so silent, it was eerie. But someone *was* on the line. Someone who had her private phone number.

Apparently the hoodlums who were after her sister knew people. Damn. She took a deep, calming breath. "I told you the money was coming. You'll get it."

Silence.

"You'll get your money."

The line went dead. Katie dialed Donna to warn her. By the time she hung up the phone again, she was ready to pace the floor. No way was she sleeping.

NEAR EIGHT the next morning, dressed in black jeans and a matching black ruffled blouse, Katie sat at Luke's island kitchen bar. With only a few hours of sleep under her belt, Katie had, nevertheless, woken up more determined than ever to keep things between her and Luke all business and, in fact, to get down to business. She placed a steamy cup of coffee beside her; she needed the caffeine and had helped herself to the coffeepot.

Those gambling sharks had to get out of her sister's life, and this job allowed Katie the financial means to make it happen. That advantage deserved grateful hard work, not the bitter resistance she'd come here with, which, if she were honest with herself, was immature and out of character.

She was here to keep the man safe, and she intended to do so. That she wanted him, that he clearly and totally rocked her body to a steamy sizzle, complicated things. But she wasn't going to allow it to get in the way of protecting him. And truth be told, playing the girlfriend put her front and center with those closest to him—and those people had to be considered suspects.

So with all that logic recapped in her mind about a million times and with her laptop fired up in front of her, Katie searched media blitzes involving Luke that might offer leads on his stalker. She tabbed through a recent story on Luke regarding the thieving, low-life manager he'd endured before Ron took over. Luke had been through some real bad stuff lately, enough to make her sit up and take notice. No wonder he didn't want Katie around, she thought, lifting her coffee cup to sip. A sudden prickling of heat tingled along her skin.

Katie's gaze lifted and settled on Luke, who was standing in the entryway, looking good enough to eat for breakfast in faded jeans, a team T-shirt that hugged his oh-so-yummy broad chest, and a pair of scuffed cowboy boots. His light brown hair, thick and a bit mussed up, screamed for well-placed female fingers—not hers, she told herself. Okay. Maybe hers.

"You're up early," he said, crossing to the coffeepot and grabbing a cup from the shiny walnut cabinet.

"So are you," she said, quickly minimizing the computer screen to hide the story she was reading so Luke wouldn't see it.

"I'm an early riser," he said from behind and to her right. "It's a curse. No matter how late I go to sleep, I wake up by eight in the morning."

She rotated around to bring him into view, resting her arm on the high back of the bar stool. "I wish I had that curse. It would make getting up easier."

"You don't want this curse. It leaves you sleep deprived more times than not." He filled his cup. "I see you found the coffee."

"Hope you don't mind," she said, but somehow she knew he didn't. "I kind of made myself at home."

He joined her at the corner of the bar, directly beside her, and reached for the creamer sitting next to her computer. "Not at all," he commented, dumping the creamer in his cup. "Nice to wake up to it already made." He snagged her spoon where it rested on a paper towel and stirred. Her spoon. He knew it was hers. It was an intimate gesture of sharing that people in relationships did and it sent a silly little flutter through Katie's stomach.

"That's what they make automatic-timer coffeepots for," she said.

He sipped his coffee. "I never seem to remember to put the coffee in the night before."

"I'm surprised Maria doesn't set it up for you," she commented.

He shrugged. "She only comes three times a week," he said. "She keeps the dust from building up while I'm gone, and it's nice to have a home-cooked meal when I've been on the road for months on end."

"Where are your parents?" Katie asked. "Are you close to them?"

"They're in Austin, Texas, where I played college ball. Still my biggest fans and the best people I have ever known in this lifetime despite being my parents."

Katie smiled softly, took a sip of her coffee. It said a lot about a man when he was not only close to his parents, but spoke openly about how close he was to them. "Any siblings?"

He took a drink and then set his cup down. "None," he said, resting his hands on the end of the island bar. "What about you? Parents? Siblings?"

She considered dodging the question, but Luke deserved to know who he was working with, especially after all she'd read about him and his past manager. "My parents died in a car crash a few years back," she said. "And yes, one sibling. A younger sister by five years who was a senior in college when it happened. And in her own words, I'm ridiculously protective of her."

He studied her a moment, and thankfully skipped the obligatory *I'm so sorry* remark that people seemed to feel the need to say and that Katie had grown to hate.

"Ron told me you'd traveled with a few high-profile musicians. Is that why you stopped? To be closer to her?"

"No," she said. "I didn't immediately come home. Nor did I see how shaken my sister was by the loss of our parents." She'd been too busy hiding from the loss herself, trying to pretend they were at home, still alive.

Until she'd found Joey with another woman and realized how much she needed a change.

Then she'd come home to discover her sister's seemingly amazing husband was a low-life user who'd gambled away Carrie's life insurance and then some.

Katie shook off the memory and continued, "My father was a retired police detective. We'd been talking about opening a private security firm together. I finally did it last year."

"You were a dancer turned security staff on tour right?"

She nodded. "Yes. And I know. It's a stretch unless you know about my father." She hesitated. "Luke. I took this job at the very last minute, and I was unprepared for our first meeting. I hadn't seen a file on your case. I still haven't, and there is no excuse for that. The truth is, I took this case as a favor to Ron, and as he, much to my embarrassment, already indicated, for financial reasons. But I want you to know, I'm good at what I do, and I understand the unique position of being in the spotlight." She inhaled and let it out, treading difficult water, uncertain how he'd respond. "This morning, I started reading through your press coverage, trying to find things that might point to your stalker. I didn't know about your manager and your ex-girlfriend trying to embezzle money from you until I read the many stories written about it. Ron should have told me. I mean—he's your manager, and he's brought this female into your life in a very intimate role. There is an uncomfortable parallel there I didn't know about. I can see why you didn't want me here. It feels unprofessional on our part, both Ron's and mine, not to address this up front. I'm prepared to make this work, but are you? I have a couple of excellent men I can recommend—"

"I want *you*, Katie," he said, his voice low but firm, his gray eyes warm. The room seemed to shrink around them, the intimacy expanding in the same breath. "No one else."

Something about the way he spoke had her body quivering. They weren't talking about security and they both knew it. "You are aware that I'm not the least bit enamored by your star-ballplayer status, right? That I won't sleep with you because you're some famous pitcher."

"I wouldn't want you if you would," he replied, his eyes holding hers, his expression unwaveringly intense.

Understanding swept through Katie as she put two and two together thanks to those articles she'd read. Luke was feeling used and abused because of his stardom. He was drawn to her for the very reasons she was nervous about him. Yet, he seemed to trust her more easily than she did him. "How do you know I'm not manipulating you?" she asked. "Maybe I'm pretending to hate athletes because that's what you want to hear?"

He stepped to her side of the bar, his big body towering over hers, her body angled toward his, her knees all that separated the two of them. He smelled fresh, of soap and shaving cream. "Because I saw how much you hated me when you thought I was like Joey last night, how much you resented Ron for bringing you here."

"And you still trust me to protect you?"

"Ron sent me your credentials, and after meeting you, I reread them. You come well qualified."

Katie believed in being direct and honest. She *liked*

that Luke was direct, as well. And she was beginning to think she liked him, too.

Feeling more than a little mesmerized by his gray eyes and nearness, she said, "All right, then. We should start working on our cover story. You know. The entire dating thing. How we met. Where we met. We should learn a few things about each other so we display convincing intimacy. Your season starts in less than a week, which thankfully is a home game. I'll want to be in the bleachers, and getting close to those close to you, so I can look for trouble."

"First things first," he said. "How do you like your eggs?" His eyes twinkled, his voice taking on a sensual play on words as he added, "Because I don't know about you, but something about all this being close stuff has me *starving*."

Katie's thighs clenched on that final word, and the implication that he was starving for more than eggs. He was starving for her. And damn it, she was starving for him. He moved to the refrigerator, and a breath escaped her lips.

Every time she brought up his security issues, he turned up the heat. Luke wasn't the only one in danger. Because she was beginning to forget why getting involved with Luke, why taking an undercover lover straight to the bedroom, was a bad thing.

AN HOUR LATER, Katie sat at the bar across from Luke, her plate pushed aside, having been lured into a game of twenty questions on the pretense of playing the roles of boyfriend and girlfriend around his team. "A Dairy

Queen Blizzard, you say." She repeated the name of his favorite ice cream treat.

He gave a decisive nod. "The best soft serve on the planet, with whatever topping you like," he said. "I prefer the chocolate-chip cookie dough."

"Dairy Queen," she repeated, crinkling her nose. "Is there a Dairy King?"

He chuckled. "Not that I know of. I'll take you to meet the Queen during the Texas series."

"If I'm still around when that time comes," she said softly, suddenly hating the fact that doing her job well meant she wouldn't be. How had she gone from damn near kneeing this man in the groin to hoping to be eating ice cream in Texas with him?

"The Texas series is coming up soon," came a male voice. "Of course you'll be around."

Katie and Luke turned at the sound of Ron's voice, finding Maria standing in the doorway beside him. He was dressed in a well-fitted black suit and tie, ready for the office.

"I came by to check on you two," Maria said, "and let him in." She glanced at the stove, where butter had spattered and been left. Crumbs decorated the counter, several jars of different jellies open beside them. "Oh, my, I hate when he cooks. He makes such a mess."

Ron's gaze flickered from Luke's to Katie's and then to Maria. He motioned them to the other room. A few seconds later, they all stood in an office, a mahogany desk as the centerpiece, surrounded by walls of sports memorabilia. Katie sat in front of the desk in a cushy leather chair. Luke sat behind it. Ron stood at one end of it, resting on the surface.

"All of Luke's mail is routed to a P.O. box," Ron said. "I picked up yesterday's on my way to work this morning." He opened a file and held up a clear bag full of a half-dozen envelopes. "I didn't open the latest one. It's the same plain envelope with no return address, stamped from another different location."

Katie glanced at Luke, who had leaned back in his chair. He shrugged, unaffected. She didn't know how he could be so nonchalant, but it appeared genuine. He really didn't feel threatened. She reached for the bag. The other five letters had all been created with cutouts from newspapers and magazines—each letter promising that Luke would die soon. She pursed her lips. "As much as I'd like to know what this new letter says, I'm sure I can guess." She fixed Luke in a hard stare, aware he wouldn't be pleased with the subject she was about to broach. "We need to get the letters examined by a crime lab."

"No police," Luke insisted. "I don't need my private life sold to the highest bidder and plastered all over the news. The entire season will become a story about my stalker instead of how the team's playing."

"Luke," she said. "I understand the press concerns. I understand your need to avoid being the newest gossip headline. I'll make sure it doesn't end up there. My men—Noah and Josh—when they get here Saturday—"

Ron interrupted, "I thought they were coming in today?"

"They were," she said. "But we took this job on short notice, and they have loose ends to tie up before they can get here. Which is unfortunate, because I really want Luke's security here at the house to be scrutinized, and Josh is an expert in that area." She turned back to Luke. "Noah is ex-FBI, Luke. He has a guy inside the FBI lab who will run the tests needed on the letters, no questions asked. No names. I promise. Let me have him make that connection for us."

She held her breath, hoping he would agree, knowing she was sending the letters to be reviewed even if he objected. No doubt Luke wanted the threats easily dismissed as nothing. But her father had always said, never ignore a gut feeling, and she had a gut feeling.

"You're sure?" Luke asked. "The lab won't ever know I'm involved?"

She nodded. "Absolutely one hundred percent sure." She glanced at Ron.

"All right, then," Luke said. "Send the letters. I'm in for anything that might end this ridiculous mess."

Katie let out a breath of relief and vowed to dig deeper with Luke. There was something behind his absolute dismissal of these threats that didn't make sense. She'd come full circle, it seemed. She wasn't bailing on Luke. She was seeing this through.

"Okay," Katie said. "We'll get the analysis done and hope for answers. In the meantime, your first game isn't until next week, and I looked at the schedule. We have six home games before you head to Texas, which is when the traveling makes the whole undercover thing almost impossible to pull off with my men. It'll have to be me traveling with you and me alone."

"My parents expect to see me when I'm in Texas," Luke said. "Either I'll have to tell them who you are or we'll have to convince them we're dating."

"Maybe Texas won't be an issue," Katie said. The idea of meeting his parents reminded her of how sleeping with Luke would complicate a situation already complicated enough. "The minute my staff arrives, we'll work fast. Maybe we can unearth your letter writer before the travel begins. The best strategy to keep you safe will be to turn this place into Fort Knox and lay low here as much as possible."

"Laying low has never been an issue for me," Luke assured her. "Right after tonight's gala at the Children's Museum."

"What gala?" Katie queried. She eyed Ron. "I really need a detailed file."

"I have it," Ron said, indicating a manila folder.

"The gala is a charity event for children's leukemia," Luke answered. "I have to be there."

"While I respect that this is a charity event," Katie said, "anything high profile is a bad idea until we get your security revamped."

"He's the emcee," Ron said. "He can't skip it. Besides, it's good for his reputation. That means endorsements and financial security we don't want to miss."

Luke's forehead furrowed. "This isn't about endorsements," he insisted. "It's about the kids." His gaze flicked to Katie. "Consider it your coming-out party. The unveiling of the woman I'm dating. In fact, I need to go pick up my tuxedo." He pushed to his feet, rounded the desk and offered her his hand. "Care to join me?"

Katie ignored his hand, more than a little aware of Ron watching them. "You're sure you can't skip this?"

"Positive," he said. "And neither can you. You're my date."

He hadn't known she was coming until yesterday. He'd been planning on going stag. Why did that please her so much?

Luke glanced at Ron. "Anything else we need to know?"

"Just that management is pleased," Ron told them. "I let them know you have security in place." He eyed Katie. "A limited number of people know the truth about your role here. Those people are all in management and motivated to protect Luke." Katie was realizing more and more that she was here to stay. She offered a brisk nod.

"I'll check in with Maria and meet you at the door in five," Luke said to Katie.

She stood up and gave him an approving look. The instant he left the room, Ron said, "Good to see the two of you getting along better."

Katie narrowed her gaze on him. "No thanks to you. Why didn't you tell me his girlfriend and ex-manager tried to embezzle money from him? I mean, under the circumstances, didn't you think that information was important? As in potential suspects?"

"I planned to tell you," he said.

"When, Ron?" she demanded, hands on her hips. "A good time to tell me would have been up front, so I was aware of all security risks without hunting them down. Not to mention, you're his manager and I'm the woman who is supposed to pretend to be his date. The comparison to his past is a parallel in some daunting ways. No wonder the man didn't want me here."

"You've been here all of twelve hours," he said. "I'm hardly delinquent in passing along information. It's in the file I brought you today. Besides, you were already trying to talk yourself out of coming here. I wasn't giving you his reasons, on top of your own. I knew once he got to know you, he'd trust you the way I do."

She studied him, shocked at how manipulative he'd been. "Too bad it's hurt my ability to trust you, Ron," she said quietly. "Leave the file on the desk. And please send an electronic copy to Donna immediately since I have this gala to attend. We should have been analyzing that data yesterday."

She turned on her heels and rushed to the door, trying to keep tabs on Luke. She charged toward the foyer, rounding a corner and rushing up the stairs. She grabbed her purse, double-checked that her gun had ammo and then headed out the bedroom door, running smack into Luke.

His hands came out to steady her. "Easy, now," he said, his strong hands resting on her arms. "Everything okay?"

"As okay as it can be considering you are stubbornly going to this gala tonight," she said, deflecting away from her conflict with Ron.

"You mean *we* are going to this gala," he said. "For the kids. You have a dress to wear?"

"Dress?" She felt the blood drain from her face. "No. I don't have a dress."

He pulled her close, surprising her as his lips caressed hers, heat flooding her limbs. "We need to find you one, then," he said. "I'm assuming you need something to hide all your secret weapons. Guns. Knives. Whatever a private security person playing the girlfriend uses to get her man. You do intend to get your man, don't you?"

Katie told herself to push him away. Ron was downstairs, and playing girlfriend didn't mean having hot sex with the client. Though, right now, hot sex with the client sounded pretty darn good. Oh, good grief, she had to get a grip.

"I'm not flirting with you, Luke," she said, shoving at his chest. It was hard, warm, sexy. She was conflicted, aroused and in trouble.

He laughed, his eyes alive with mischief. "But you want to and that's a good start. We'll work on the follow-through while we find you that dress." He grabbed her hand and pulled her behind him, but there was no question he was the one in pursuit.

She decided right then and there she'd need to re-address the boundaries between them. He could not seduce her into dismissing her duty, and she suspected that was his plan.

He needed to be clear on one thing—she would not be distracted by sex. But as the warm heat of his hand over hers slid up her arms, she conceded she might have to allow herself a private fantasy or two. But then Luke didn't have to know that little detail.

5

KATIE CAME OUT of the dressing room of the swanky clothing store to find Luke sitting in the chair outside the door. His gaze swept her jeans-clad body with intimate perusal before lifting to her face. "I thought I was helping you pick your dress."

She motioned to the black chiffon number in her hand that hit right above the knee, with sequins on the straps that wrapped around her neck. "I already picked."

"You only tried on three dresses," he said. "I thought you women normally had to try on twenty or thirty to find 'the one.'"

Katie glanced toward the fifty-something store attendant, who was helping another customer. "This is business. I needed a dress. I found a dress." And, boy, had she gotten lucky. Normally, she *could* try on twenty or thirty dresses to find a good one. "We need to get back to your place and recap our cover story."

He studied her, making no move to get up from the chair before finally standing and stepping close to her. "I know it's business and all, Katie," he said, "but you might as well enjoy the night." His voice softened, tenderness caressing its depths. "Get a dress you like."

The intimacy that came so easily between them rattled Katie. It was something she'd never experienced with a man. Maybe it was his Southern, good-guy charm that Ron had sworn existed, hidden in their first encounter but flourishing now.

Whatever it was, it was warming her inside and out. Impairing her ability to think straight and do her job. She should be scanning for trouble, not staring into those silvery-gray eyes of his. "I like the dress," she managed, though even to her own ears her voice was low, affected.

He reached up and brushed her hair over her shoulder. "You're sure?"

His touch was electric, fire on her skin. Goose bumps lifted on her neck. Oh, man. Why couldn't he have kept up that jerk routine. It really would have made this assignment easier if she hated him. Because she didn't hate him anymore. She *really* did not hate him. "Yes," she said. "I'm sure."

He paused, as if assessing her sincerity, and then said, "Good, then let's seal the deal and make it ours." He reached for the dress.

Katie frowned and moved away, pulling the dress out of reach. "What are you doing?"

"I'm going to pay for it."

"Oh, no," she said quickly. "You are *not* buying my dress."

Surprise flashed in his face before his jaw set. "You need it because of my party. I'm buying it."

She tried to step around him. "I don't need you to

buy me a dress." It made her feel for sale. It made her feel...bad.

He maneuvered in front of her. "Katie. I'm buying the dress."

"No. You are not."

He grimaced. "You wouldn't need this dress if not for my function tonight. Technically, isn't it a work expense?"

That idea ground along her nerve endings like sandpaper on wood. Right. Work. Not a date. Not that she'd ever thought it was. Not that she wanted it to be. She shoved the dress at him more abruptly than intended and responded in a tone more agitated than intended. "Fine. You can buy the dress. I'll be at the front of the store waiting."

She got a glimpse of his confused face but didn't stay for a full-on inspection. She rushed away, no idea why she was upset.

A few minutes later, Luke joined her at the doorway. She didn't look at him, instead scanning the surrounding areas for anything that indicated danger. He held the door for her as she climbed into his Ford Explorer.

Once he was inside, doors shut, he didn't start the engine. "I've decided you're a very complicated woman. You didn't want me to buy the dress. Then when I tried to make you feel okay about me buying it, I said something wrong."

"You didn't say anything wrong, Luke." Luke, resting his arm on the steering wheel, turned to study her more closely.

"I'm assuming that translates to mean I didn't say anything wrong, but I didn't say anything right, either."

Katie cut her gaze, staring out of the front window. She didn't confirm or deny his assessment, though he was right on target. She'd had some sort of meltdown inside she had yet to understand. She wanted Luke to be like Joey, buying everyone and everything—a jerk, easy to dismiss. Then she didn't want him to be like Joey. She wanted him to be a real good guy.

The heat of Luke's inspection sizzled along her skin, and Katie decided a subject change was her best response. "With the shopping behind us, we can get back to work." She glanced in his direction. "I need to review the data in the file Ron gave us today, including a detailed rundown of your relationships, past and present, good and bad, so I can begin ruling out people close to you being responsible for these letters. Unfortunately, and uncomfortably, that means your ex-girlfriend and ex-manager, as well." And his present manager, Katie thought. Not that she suspected Ron of anything. He'd hired her after all, but she wasn't excluding him. The Ron she thought she knew would never have manipulated her and Luke as he had recently.

"Got it," Luke said. "You changed the subject. Now it's my turn. I'm changing the subject." He turned the ignition over. "I have to be in my monkey suit and at the charity event for a photo call at five and it's already pushing one o'clock. I'd suggest we grab a bite to eat and plan your coming-out party."

She frowned and reached for his arm, stopping him from putting the truck into gear. Awareness shot through her body; she swallowed hard, pulling her hand back, and tried again. Luckily, she sounded composed. "You aren't taking these threats seriously," she accused.

"Those letters might seem silly to you, but anyone who goes to enough trouble to cut out words from newspapers and magazines and then mail them off, changing postmarks each time, is meticulous, smart and unstable. That's a bad combination. So please, don't ignore these letters."

His hand dropped from the gearshift as he angled his body toward hers. "I'm not ignoring the letters, just the idea of a real threat behind them. I'm of the opinion someone is trying to rattle my cage—or rather, my game. There's a lot of ugly jealousy and competition in this sport. Hell, in all sports. We like to pretend it doesn't exist, but it does."

"Don't you think threatening letters are pretty extreme?" she asked.

"And taking steroids that might damage your body and get you kicked out of the game isn't?"

She inclined her head. "Point taken."

"And since we're breaking this down. That salt-in-the-water incident—that would have been laughed off as a team prank under different circumstances, but one of the letters made it to the management office."

"Ron didn't mention that," Katie said.

"Well, good thing I did, then," he said, "considering it's a fairly important detail. In other words, someone wanted them breathing down my throat."

"Even if this person is trying to rattle you, Luke," Katie warned, "you have to see this is unstable behavior." Sooner or later, the guilty party would step up their game, do more than letters and salt in the water.

"Maybe," he conceded. "But whoever this is, they aren't bringing me down. I won't let them. I have a zone

I enter when I walk onto that mound, and nothing but the game exists there. And I had a damn good preseason to prove it."

Understanding filled Katie. "I remember that zone," she said softly, drawing his surprised look. "When I was dancing, before I blew out my knee, everything else disappeared inside the music and the routine."

He stared at her for a long moment. "You loved dancing. That was your real dream. Not this security biz."

She gave a terse nod. "Yes. My dancing was your baseball. I was injured and I knew it, but I landed a choreographer spot on a top musician's tour. *The top spot.*" She remembered the call all too well. "I'd been a nobody so long. It was my big break."

"And you blew out your knee again," he murmured.

"Right. Messed it up for good." She tilted her head acceptingly. "But that's old news. I've adjusted and moved on. What else can I do? What can any of us do in such a situation?"

Katie settled her leg on the seat and turned to face him. "The point in my story, Luke, isn't about me. It's about you. I want you to know I understand where you're coming from. I don't want you to feel I'm working against your career. I know the first game of the season is less than a week away. I can see why it's important you don't let this mess with your head, and I'll do everything in my power to make the security fade into the background. To let you play. In fact, if you're right and someone is trying to mess with your head, it will be my great pleasure to watch you pitch the best season of your career."

A slow smile slid onto his lips. "I *am* going to pitch the best season of my career."

"And I'll be here covering your back while you do," she promised, returning his smile.

His gaze lowered to her lips, lingered, then lifted. "What would you do if I grabbed you and kissed you right now?"

"You don't want to know," she warned, trying to keep the playful out of her tone, but it was hard. So hard.

His eyes lit with desire. "What if I do?"

What if she did, too? "Drive the truck."

She'd barely finished issuing the order when he pulled her close, that big, hard body touching her in all the right places. His tongue thrusting deep into her mouth in a long, drugging kiss. She tried to seem unaffected, but he tasted so good, felt too perfect. She could feel the moan rising in her throat; she willed it back. But it was there, escaping her lips and declaring the blissful state of arousal overtaking her body.

Luke smiled against her mouth. "I had a feeling that's what you'd do."

She shook herself inwardly and shoved out of his arms. "That's not what I should have done. I should have punished you in some horrible, painful way involving my knee."

"You and that knee." He chuckled and put the truck in gear. "I'm sure you can think of a way to punish me that doesn't include *horrible* and *painful* in the description."

Erotic images about how she might punish him—tie him up, kiss every one of his delicious abdominals and elsewhere while he begged for more. Oh, boy. Katie shook herself, but judging from Luke's renewed rumble of deep, sexy laughter, not before he guessed she was in naughty land.

Katie glared at him and snatched her seat belt, doing the only safe thing the truck allowed. She secured herself as far from Luke as possible for as long as possible—until tonight, when she was destined to be on his arm, as his date. Protecting him. Now, who the heck was going to protect her from him? That was the real question. And did she really want to be?

THE PHOTO CALL CAME in the blink of an eye, a large banquet-type hotel room set up as a studio. He'd barely arrived before he'd been whisked into the center of attention. After what felt like hours of pictures, Luke escaped the photographers and headed for the sidelines where Katie stood patiently waiting.

Crazy as it seemed, he was hot and hard, just thinking of touching her, of inhaling her sweet floral scent. Damn. The woman had him all shaken and stirred in a big way. She was a challenge. It was the only logical explanation. She wasn't falling at his feet. She didn't want him for his game. She didn't even want to want him.

Yeah, it was the challenge getting to him, he confirmed in his mind. It was the only damn explanation he was willing to accept. Because there was no way in hell he was falling for this woman, or any other, having had his heart twisted in knots only months before. Not that he'd ever really loved his ex. A detail made clear when he'd missed his manager more than he'd missed Rebecca. The man had been with him since the day he'd been drafted out of college, almost ten years ago now. Rebecca had been with him a year, but nevertheless, she'd been a stable comfort in his life, one that didn't come easily with a decade of traveling under his belt.

Katie smiled as he approached—a genuine smile that seemed to say she was glad he was headed in her direction—and it lit him up like the sun beaming down on the pitcher's mound on a hot summer afternoon. She'd been around high society and public figures before, and it showed in how smoothly she managed interaction with several people far more famous than he'd ever dreamed of being. She wasn't all starry-eyed and infatuated. Damn if she wasn't a breath of fresh air. He liked it. And he definitely liked how she looked in the slim-cut black dress she'd chosen. It hugged her slender, athletic body exactly the way he would want it to—tastefully close—at least for now. Later, if he was lucky, he'd explore her long, slender legs in delicious, intimate detail.

He stopped in front of her, slid a hand to her waist. "How are you hanging in there?"

"Displeased with the event's security," she replied. "If this wasn't for a good cause, I would have you out of here in a snap."

His other hand settled on her waist. "I don't know if I've ever been with a woman so hell-bent on control." He wiggled an eyebrow. "I think I like it."

"You're not *with me*," she reminded him, hushing her voice. "I'm protecting you."

He leaned close, inhaled. "You smell like spring flowers." The scent zipped through his system with a rush of heat. "Remind me to thank Ron for manipulating me into *not* being with you."

She slid her fingers down his lapel, her breath warm on his neck as she leaned in and whispered, "Not unless you tell me it's because you feel safer now, because that's why I'm here. To keep you safe."

"You talk so tough," he accused. "But I think you're all soft and warm underneath all that toughness."

She gave him a disbelieving look and shook her head. "Soft and warm?" Her voice quavered ever so slightly, not quite as controlled as normal. "I told you I don't like baseball—actually, I told you I don't like *you*. What part of either of those things sounds soft and warm?"

"Both," he assured her. "Because you didn't mean either one of them. And for the record, *safe* isn't the word that comes to mind where you're concerned." He threw her the zinger on purpose, looking forward to her swatting it back at him. This woman was definitely something. "On a separate subject. I've had a burning question on my mind the entire time I was taking pictures."

"Burning?" she said. "Do I dare ask?"

He didn't give her a chance to decide. "Where exactly," he whispered, leaning down, his mouth near her ear, "do you keep your gun in this dress?"

"Luke." Her hand flattened on his chest. "Will you please behave?"

His hand closed over hers, pinning it against his body, where he wanted it, where he wanted her. Soon. Not soon enough. "Answer my question, and I promise to be good. For a while. If you really want me to."

She tried to glare at him but erupted in a smile

instead. "Like I said, you're impossible. And no, I won't tell you. A girl has her secrets."

"And a man, his fantasies," he countered, wondering if it was strapped beneath a garter. Was she wearing thigh-highs? "I'm going to be thinking about where to find that gun all night, you know?"

"Oh, good," came a female voice. "There you are."

Luke cringed at the sound of the voice behind him and turned.

"Olivia," he said, acknowledging the PR rep whom the team owner had hired after Luke's embezzlement scandal had rocked the headlines. "I didn't expect you tonight. I thought a charity event would have been good enough press without your help." His hand stayed possessively at Katie's back. Olivia was a money-grubbing fame mogul, like so many women he'd encountered in the past ten years. "Katie. This is Olivia Cantu. She's—"

"The Rainmaker," Olivia supplied, her normal, big ego in play. An ego that matched her ample cleavage, exposed within a millimeter of being unprofessional. "I'm the one who spins all the stories into jewels rather than media-shattering craters." She cast Katie a look down her nose. "Would you be my latest crater?"

"I'd be Katie Lyons," Katie said, taking the impolite comment impressively in stride. "Luke's date…and I'd prefer to be neither a jewel nor a crater, thus why I rarely attend these events."

Olivia frowned. "You make that sound like you've been around awhile." Her gaze shifted suspiciously toward Luke.

"She's been my jewel in hiding for some time now,

Olivia. I didn't want her exposed to the nightmare of my bad press."

Olivia gave Katie a judgmental up-and-down inspection that oozed jealousy before fixing her attention on Luke again, speaking as if Katie were not present.

"The press'll be talking about this new date of yours," she said, flipping a long lock of blond hair out of her heavily made-up eye. "After that disaster with your last girlfriend, I need something to work with here." She glanced at Katie. "I'm sorry." She didn't sound sorry. "But we don't need another catastrophe. I need to know who I'm dealing with."

Instantly, Luke felt the subtle stiffening of Katie's back. Olivia was supposed to stop problems from occurring, not create them. And damn it, he reveled in the competitiveness of his sport on the field, but off the field, he was sick of the jealousy and competition. The game wasn't about the fancy team jet, or who had the most groupies, or who drove what car, yet plenty of people made it about all those things and more.

In that moment, Luke respected and appreciated how untouched Katie was by all of the bullshit around him, despite having rubbed elbows with plenty of celebrities in her past.

Protectiveness for Katie rose inside him, and yes, a selfish need to keep her untouched that he didn't deny. "There is absolutely nothing about Katie to worry about, Olivia," he said through clenched teeth. "For once, try simply answering with 'no comment,' or how about this? Tell them I'm crazy hot for Katie. Take that to the press and let them roll with it. Or I'll do it myself." He grabbed Katie's hand and started walking.

Olivia and Katie both gasped. Olivia stepped in front of them. "Luke—don't go saying crazy things to the press just to spite me," Olivia said. "Wilcox won't be happy about that." Wilcox being the team owner.

He arched a brow. "Why would I have any reason to spite you, Olivia?"

She opened her mouth and shut it. Then, "Just watch what you say."

He glanced at Katie. "Let's go find a table." They headed down a narrow, carpeted hallway, and Luke cast Katie a furtive glance. "I'm sorry."

"I've dealt with my share of Olivias," she assured him, keeping pace with him. "And for the record, I thought of a good five or ten biting remarks for that woman and said not a one of them, but you might have gone a bit far with the *crazy hot* thing."

He stopped, turned to her. "It was the truth."

Surprise washed over her face and she visibly paled. "Luke. No. Stop. Don't you understand? I can't protect you when you're making me..."

"Crazy hot?"

"Crazy," she corrected quickly. "You're making me crazy."

His lips tilted upward. "Then I'll get to work on the wild-and-hot part."

A flash of light suddenly flickered around them, the sound of voices as reporters swarmed them. Katie quipped, "I'd say the 'hot' is safely on ice considering there's an audience."

He winked. "Don't count on it, sweetheart."

AN HOUR LATER, Luke had finished a heart-wrenching speech that told Katie there was so much more to him than she'd imagined possible. And while he was sign-ing autographs, she worked the crowd, looking for suspects.

At present she danced with Chris Allen, a thirty-something, money-grubbing sports agent whom she'd known for years. Listening to him rattle his own chain and tell her how much Luke Winter and Joey Martin needed him—no matter how many times she assured him she had no influence over either—was pure torture. Good grief, she was ready to leave. The party and this world.

She'd forgotten how easily every breath she drew had been about Joey when she'd been with him. And how much Joey had eaten that up, too. He'd loved being the center of the universe. And she'd done nothing but feed his ego, and his desires. She'd come to hate Joey, though she hadn't realized it until months after their separation, when she'd finally rediscovered herself.

She'd like to think she'd grown since then, that she was older, more capable of retaining her own identity with a man like Luke than she had been before. That—if Luke wasn't a client and off-limits—she could be with him without losing her identity. Part of her was tempted to find out. Another wanted to leave the past in the past.

"Can I cut in?"

The male voice that lifted above the jazz tune came with both relief and trepidation, as Chris turned his at-tention on Luke. Immediately, Chris's eyes lit up, and he reached in his pocket, withdrew a card. "We should talk." He beamed. "Katie and I go way back."

Luke ignored the card. "Tonight is for the kids, man,"

Luke said, disapproval on his face. "No business." He slid his arms around Katie, turned her in to the mix of the dancing couples.

"Thank you," Katie said, her gaze flickering to those sparkling gray eyes and quickly away. It would be so easy to get lost in his stare. "I can't stand that man."

"Good," Luke said, his legs brushing hers, his body warm and inviting. "Because neither can I. He can't seem to get the idea that I'm not interested."

"Wait," Katie said, her fingers digging into his jacket. "How long has he been pursuing you? Since before the letters started?"

He paused a minute and then spun her around. "You think Chris is writing the letters?" he asked in disbelief.

The soft, gentle rhythm of their bodies moving together fogged Katie's brain for a second, the sway of his hips against hers making it hard to think. "Maybe," she said, gently clearing her throat. "What if he wants to destroy your career so he can recreate it? We both know he's willing to do whatever's necessary to get ahead. He's that type. It has to be considered." Just as Olivia was possibly looking to create juicy gossip that made her, and her job, necessary, as well. Or Olivia might simply want Luke period. Katie could see her as an obsessive stalker, but she didn't say that for fear Luke would accuse her of sounding jealous. She wasn't jealous, because really, truthfully, there was something not right about that girl that reached beyond her silicone double-D breasts and too-perfect body. Both Chris and Olivia were going on the list of people Katie had begun compiling for Donna to investigate.

A flash of a camera, and Katie and Luke were once again being photographed. Luke grimaced at the camera holder. "I know that guy," he said. "He's with some low-life gossip magazine." He maneuvered her farther onto the crowded dance floor. "No matter how grand the cause, the wolves and cameras are out in full force. It can't just be about the kids."

"You didn't seem to mind the cameras and the spotlight earlier," she said skeptically. "You worked the room like you owned it up on that stage."

"Every minute I'm in front of the cameras is like tying a string to a tooth and slamming a door," he said. "Painful."

"Yet you play pro ball. In front of thousands. On national television...you're always in the spotlight."

"I love baseball," he said. "And the spotlight is a part of competing on a professional level. But I'm a country boy at heart. I like quiet. I like privacy. Until all that crap with my manager, you never saw me in the papers. I spend my time off away from the limelight. The cameras, the fancy parties—I don't want anything to do with them unless I have to." His hand slid more intimately around her back, her stomach fluttering with reaction. He tilted his head, studied her. "You seem surprised."

Maybe she was. She didn't know what to expect from Luke. Ron had said Luke was a good ol' boy. A private, nice, down-to-earth guy. Then, Ron had introduced her to a big, egomaniac jerk. Which one was accurate? Which was a show?

"You're emcee tonight," she said, trying to find an answer to that question. "That hardly seems like avoiding the limelight."

His expression darkened, the flutter of overhead lights casting his face in shadows. "For one reason and one reason only," he said. "And that reason is Elvin Rogers. A kid that had one last wish—to meet me."

Katie stopped dancing, her heart in her chest. "Did you? Meet him?"

He nodded. "Yeah. I met him. I was with him the day he died."

Respect for Luke she hadn't thought possible the night before expanded inside her. "Oh, Luke. I'm so sorry." She'd told herself she'd put the past behind her before meeting Luke, but then she'd judged him by his career, which was wrong. That didn't mean he was some crown prince, but it meant, from now on, he deserved to be judged for who he was, not for her expectations of who he was.

"Excuse me." Suddenly, Rick Raundo, the Italian-American right fielder on Luke's team, was by their side. He was tall and dark, with a nose that was a bit on the large side and a sense of humor even larger. Katie liked him instantly and had talked to him through much of dinner. "They want Luke here for one last photo op," Rick said, his hand coming down on Luke's shoulder. "Grin and bear it, man. It's with the president of the Leukemia Association." Rick smiled at Katie. "I'll stay behind and defend Katie from any media attacks."

Luke grimaced and cast Katie a warning look. "Watch out for his wandering hands," he said, and leaned close. "We'll escape right after I finish up." He surprised her by kissing her, a short, sweet caress of the lips, and he was gone before she could stop him.

Rick immediately turned his attention to Katie. But

this wasn't the Rick from dinner, all full of laughter and jokes.

"Look, Katie," he said, his tone dark, his expression darker. "You seem like a nice person, and I get that you're here to protect Luke and all. But don't go getting him all worked up over these letters and screwing with his game. Baseball is everything to Luke."

For the second time, Katie found herself blindsided. "Excuse me?"

"Do your job and beyond, for all I care," Rick said. *Beyond* implying sex, without question. "But don't try to freak Luke out."

"Go back to the 'while you're protecting him' part," she ground out between her teeth, ignoring the couple crowding them. "What does that mean?"

"I know who you are," he said. "He told me you—"

"Don't!" she said, poking a finger at his chest. "Do not say it out loud. Don't say it to anyone. Do you hear me?"

She was already storming away from Rick. Luke wasn't supposed to tell anyone who she was or why she was here. She was furious with him. She couldn't protect him when he wasn't cooperating. And she couldn't protect him when she kept thinking about getting him naked, either.

Rick caught up with her quickly. "Katie, dammit."

She motioned him to a corner, away from the crowd.

"I want you to think about this," Rick said, his voice low, terse. "But if someone is trying to ruin Luke's career, bringing you in here to make this into a big deal is only making it worse."

The only thing keeping Katie from wringing Rick's neck was that she believed he had good intentions, no matter how misplaced. He was worried about Luke.

"I'm here to protect him, Rick, and yes, those letters might be about messing with his head and his game and that's it, but—"

"What else could it be?" Rick challenged.

"If you're wrong and there's a real threat," Katie said, "Luke could get hurt. Is that what you want? Luke dead because you were protecting his career?"

"Oh, man, Katie," Rick said. "The 'dead' card is unfair."

"So is the 'guilt' card," Katie countered.

He scrubbed his jaw. "All I'm asking is that you keep whatever you do low-key with Luke. Be as intense as you want when he's not around, but let him stay focused on his game."

"What's going on, you two?" Luke said, walking up beside them.

"Katie?" Rick asked urgently, ignoring Luke.

She shook her head. "I'll do my best."

Rick nodded. "I'm out of here," he said to Luke. "See you later, man."

Luke frowned. "Do your best at what?" he asked Katie.

She tilted her chin up. "Is there anyone else who knows who I am that I should be aware of, Luke?"

He scanned the room for Rick, who'd already pulled a disappearing act, and then turned his attention back at Katie. "I can explain—"

"Is there anyone else?"

"No."

"Can we leave now?"

He opened his mouth to speak and then shut it. "Kissing you wouldn't solve anything, would it?"

"Besides getting you that knee you've been asking for?" she challenged. "Nope."

"It might be worth it," he said, his hand reaching for her.

"Or it might just give Olivia something to explain to the press. I'd love to see how she spins it—'New girlfriend knees Luke Winter in the groin, swears she tripped and fell.'"

He gave one long nod. "No kiss."

Her agreement was instant. "No kiss."

They started walking, and he leaned closer. "I think we should talk about this in the truck."

"You can drive," she said. "I'll talk." It was time for Luke Winter to understand this was business and she was in control. The kisses would have to wait until this assignment was over, and she planned to tell him so.

As soon as they were safely tucked inside Luke's truck, away from the crowd, Katie began her lecture, and Luke took his verbal bashing in silence, for the most part. He didn't believe for a minute that she didn't want him to kiss her again, nor did he believe they could be together and not do so. To pretend otherwise was setting them both up for problems better avoided.

With that in mind, the moment they were inside his front door and he'd flipped on the security system, Luke quickly grabbed her hand, even as she headed for her escape, toward the stairs. A moment later he was leaning against the front door with her in his arms, and before she could object, he slid his fingers into the silky mass of her hair as he'd longed to do all night.

"Pretending to date and leaving out the kissing isn't going to work." And with that announcement, he kissed her, a deep, passionate kiss that he wanted to have go on and on—as in all night. Maybe beyond. He couldn't get enough of this woman. Not of her taste or the soft, sweet moans she made when he kissed her just right—which was apparently now.

Luke was about sixty seconds from picking her up and carrying her to his room when he forced himself to end the kiss. "That's why it won't work. Because both of us like it too much." He took a step away from her. "You're supposed to be dating me. So date me. Focus on meeting the people around me and decide who is trustworthy and who is not, rather than what you should or should not be doing with me. And let your staff do the high-tech security stuff."

She swallowed hard. "It's not that simple and you know it."

"It is that simple," he insisted. "Sleep on it, Katie. Think about it before your staff gets here. We'll talk tomorrow." He stepped around her and headed up the stairs in search of a cold shower, or maybe two.

6

KATIE TOSSED and turned in Luke's big, empty, spare bed. Luke's bed. That was what kept popping into her head. Luke's house. Luke's bed. Luke's mockery of a girlfriend. Her desire for that man was *mocking her*.

She sat up, her cotton gown rasping over her bare breasts, the friction chasing a path straight to her core. Good grief, she was losing her mind and it was Luke's fault. It had been a lifetime since she'd had sex, and then he'd come along and kissed her. And Donna hadn't helped. Now she couldn't stop conjuring images of Luke's nice, tight backside in his baseball pants. Or better yet—without them. Him on top of her, naked, a nice mirror over the top of them, while he flexed those steely buns, buried inside her.

Katie fell back against the pillows, her body flushed with desire. How was she going to deal with Luke's advances when it was all she could do to keep from orgasming just thinking about the man. She swallowed. "You take the edge off yourself, Katie," she whispered. Right. Like that was going to work. Then again, lying here fighting the need wasn't going to work, either.

Her lashes lowered and she began unbuttoning the front of her gown. Giving in to the need for a good fantasy. And though she doubted seriously that any amount of fantasizing would satisfy her desire for Luke, she had to try. She had a job to do. Lusting after the man she was protecting was a distraction she didn't need.

So she wouldn't lust. Or she would. Right here and now in bed. But that's all she would allow herself. Starting with a fantasy about that magic tongue of his. Her hands traveled to her breasts, over her nipples. Oh, yeah, they needed that tongue. Lots of licks, lots of kisses. Lots of hotness.

Her eyes went to the ceiling. What if there was a mirror there? Why didn't people put mirrors above the bed? She blinked, imagined it there. Again, imagined Luke's nice bum. Her hands traveled along her body, slid between her legs, fingers gliding over sensitive flesh as she dreamed of Luke pumping into her, his backside flexing. She squeezed her eyes shut. Seeing it. Feeling it in the ache growing between her thighs.

If only he were here, stretching her. Taking her. The ache was building, the pleasure thrumming through her. Suddenly, too soon, way too soon, Katie shattered, her body quaking with the much-needed release.

Chest heaving, she turned her head to the clock. Oh, wow. "Katie, you're pathetic." She'd come in four minutes flat. And rather than consider how extraordinarily badly that spoke of her sex life, or lack thereof, Katie found herself wondering instead about Luke. Could the real man make her come that fast? Would she want him to? Katie laughed. Of course, she would. As long as he made her come again right after.

It was a thought that turned dangerously in the wrong direction fifteen minutes later, when Luke's suggestion that she simply give in to her temptation to be with him started sounding good. Katie decided self-satisfaction was not the way to get over this lusty want for Luke. Instead, she decided she'd hit the track surrounding Luke's property, and donned her shorts and running shoes.

That he, too, was obviously a runner didn't help matters; she didn't need anything they had in common bouncing around in her head right now. She took the stairs with tentative, soft footsteps, careful not to wake Luke. This was a good opportunity to check out the cameras on the grounds anyway—analyze where they were positioned and where she might suggest her team place new ones. She'd seen enough of his limited security system to know that an upgrade was an absolute must.

Katie turned off the alarm system long enough to slip out the back patio door, a rainbow of colors streaking the early morning sky as the sun began to break what had been a pitch-black horizon. She loved this—simply going to the backyard to take a run rather than taking the subway to Central Park as she usually did at home. Katie stretched first and with her iPod attached to her hip she weaved through a courtyard, complete with pool and hot tub, and found the edge of the track.

And then she was off, running but not escaping her thoughts. Donna's words bounced around in her head as readily as the memory of Luke's lips on hers, his powerful arms around her. And though Katie was so completely over Joey he wasn't even a consideration, Donna's lecture that Katie had not moved on held some truth. Because the impact of what she'd been through with him was far from gone.

Katie needed to get over her fear of being hurt as much as she needed to get over her prejudice. She'd judged Luke unfairly—if Luke was a jerk, he deserved to earn that label all by himself, like any guy. But working through those feelings while on an assignment didn't seem smart, though Ron had all but handed Luke to her on a silver platter—and handed *her* to Luke. They were both on the rebound from a nasty past. Both perhaps were using that "silver platter" to push the past, to the past. Katie wasn't sure if that was a good thing or a bad thing.

Rocks outlined the path, fancy spotlights nestled between them, illuminating her path and allowing her to inspect the area, but as she cut a corner while noting a camera not properly rotating, she suddenly blasted into a hard object.

Katie gasped as she was knocked off her feet and hit the ground, scraping her leg down one of the light fixtures as she landed. Pain shot through her leg, but Katie instinctively rolled, assuming attack, ready to fight. She was in a squatting position, her palms bracing her weight when she brought Luke into focus, towering above her, hands on his hips, breathing heavily.

"Shit," he mumbled under his breath as he knelt down in front of her. "Katie, are you all right? I'm sorry. I didn't expect anyone else to be out here." He reached out and steadied her, his hands on her bare thighs. "You're bleeding."

Instant awareness raced through her body. His broad, well-chiseled chest evident in his snug T-shirt, his hands warm on her legs. Her mind was still a cluttered mess that left her body in control. And her body wanted Luke.

"I... I'm fine," she said, summoning her voice, and some mental wherewithal. "Why are you out here in the first place?" She started to stand up, and realized blood was gushing down her leg. "Damn." Still, she wanted to make her point. "You have to tell the person responsible for your security before you go running around in the dark. That person would be me. That's a new rule. You have to follow it."

"You need stitches, Katie," he said, ignoring her rule, as he did all the others, which she would have complained about, yelled even, if not for what he did next. Luke ripped his shirt over his head, his broad chest bared to display rippling muscle and a sprinkle of light brown, mouthwatering hair. "Sit," he ordered. "I need to tie off the wound to stop the bleeding."

So, aside from itsy-bitsy running shorts, the man was naked. Almost gloriously, wonderfully naked. "You'll ruin your shirt," she insisted. "And I'm fine. Just grab me some paper towels before we go in the door so I don't get blood on your floor."

"Sit down and let me do this, or I will *sit* you down, Katie," Luke said, fixing her in a steady stare. "Don't be stubborn."

She inhaled, still breathless from her run, and sat down. He wiped off the cut, his head tilted down to study the gash along the side of her calf, which didn't worry her nearly as much as the throbbing of her bad knee. She knew the routine well. Ice and lots of it. Pain reliever. Lots of it. Take it easy for a day.

"It's deep," Luke said. "Have you had a tetanus shot lately?"

"Yes," she replied. "What I need is up." And away from his bare chest and temptation, so she could tend to her knee. "Tie the shirt or whatever you are going to do and let me get up, please. I'm feeling claustrophobic." Translation—hot—for him.

"We should go to the E.R.," he said, doing as she wished, tying his shirt around her leg.

"Not a chance," she said. "I'll be fine." She pushed to her feet. Her damn knee wobbled, and Luke caught her a second before she was going down. Pain rocketed up her thigh. She rested her head on his shoulder. "Not now," she murmured, emotion wrenching her chest the way the tendons were her leg.

Inhaling through the pain, she cursed the vulnerability that her knee created. She was going to have to have help getting inside, but it felt bigger than that. She'd spent the past year working to be strong, to deal with losing her parents and to help her sister do the same, and her new career had offered a positive way to do that. And now her sister was in trouble and the assignment she was on, which would get her out of that trouble, was fast tumbling into disaster. She glanced up at Luke, holding on to his arm. "It's my knee, Luke. But I'm supposed to be taking care of you, and—"

"Why don't we take turns?" he suggested, his arm wrapping around her waist, a solid foundation that was comforting and secure. The fingers of his free hand slid under her chin. "I'll take care of you now. You can take care of me later?"

Something about the way he looked at her, the way he

said those words, made her melt inside. It was definite: Luke got to her in a big way. Though she was quite certain that right now, in pain, with him shirtless and holding her, was not the time to make any conclusions about how to deal with their relationship, or lack thereof. Especially since in that moment, she really could not bear the idea of never kissing this man again.

"Okay, then," she conceded. "I just need to lean on you to get inside." Suddenly, she was gasping as she was scooped up in his arms. "What are you doing, Luke?"

"Letting you lean on me," he said. "Now let's get you to the E.R." He was already walking toward the house.

"No!" she blurted, clinging to his neck. "No E.R. I just need ice, something to kill the pain and a bandage. That's all. I'll be fine. It's too close to your first game for us to be in the E.R. rather than dealing with the reason I'm here—those letters."

Luke keyed the security code, shoved open the door to the kitchen and set Katie down at the informal dining table. He quickly grabbed another chair to prop her leg up on.

"I'm going to get blood on the chair."

"I don't care about the damn chair, Katie," he said, lifting his shirt and checking her wound. "You're going to the E.R."

"No, I—"

He lifted the shirt all the way off and wiped the wound, which filled with blood instantly, but not before she saw the huge gash. "Okay," she agreed in frustration. The cut was deeper than she'd thought. The pain in her knee had overshadowed the rest. "I'll go to the E.R."

She motioned to his bare chest and long, muscular legs. "But you might want to consider putting some clothes on first."

He tied his shirt back around her leg. "I'd really hoped to have you ordering me to take my clothes off, not telling me to put them back on."

"It must be a sign," she said. "You're meant to keep them on."

"I don't believe in signs," he assured her. "Just hard work. I've always worked hard for what I want." He leaned down and kissed her hurt knee. "And I want you, Katie."

A LITTLE PAST EIGHT in the morning, with Katie lying down in the passenger seat sleeping and a new day's sunshine already promising to be scorching hot, Luke pulled his truck into his driveway and parked.

Though he wasn't one to throw his weight around and ask for special privileges, when he was given the chance to slip Katie into a private E.R. room for fast attention, neither of them had complained. She had six stitches in her calf and a swollen knee she refused to have X-rayed, insisting no E.R. would be able to help her. He hadn't been inclined to disagree. It was a chronic problem, and she needed a specialist. Being that she wasn't at home near her regular doctor, Luke intended to lend her the team doc later in the day. For now, he wanted to get them both some rest.

Katie sat up and stretched, a moan following that she tried to hide. "I guess that pain pill they gave me knocked me out," she said. "I hate those damn things."

He chuckled. "That doesn't surprise me." She'd been

unable to watch them stitch her leg, but she'd asked for a second-by-second explanation of what was happening. She was a control freak in the worst way. "Stay put and I'll come around and help you."

Of course she didn't. He'd barely made it to the hood of the truck to come around the vehicle, and already she had her door open.

Luke rushed to her side and stopped her from getting out. "You don't listen," he complained, and wrapped his arm around her to pick her up.

"I can walk," she said, her hand pressing to his chest to push him away, her mouth so damn close to his.

He kissed her, a soft brush of his lips over hers that was inviting and sent blood right to his groin. "We both know your knee is far more an issue than those stitches," he said. "You're exhausted and in pain. Stop beating yourself up for being human." He brushed his knuckle over her cheek. "I'm going to carry you inside and get you some ice for that knee so you can sleep this off. Once you're back to normal, you can be in charge again. Fair enough?"

"You said 'I'm in charge,' so I'm going to hold you to that."

Luke lifted her. "I think I might enjoy that," he teased, and kicked the door shut then started walking.

"Wait!" she said. "Lock the truck."

He gave her an *are you crazy* look. "My hands are full."

"We have to lock it, Luke."

"I'll come back and lock it, once you're inside."

"No, you won't," she accused.

"You're right," he said, taking the stairs to the front

door. "I won't." He slid her down his body, unlocked the front door, and then pointed the keys at the truck and hit the automatic lock. His eyebrow inched upward. "Happy?"

"I just want you to be safe," she said, as he helped her in the door and shut it, keying the security code into the panel.

"Stop worrying about me," he ordered.

"It's my job, Luke."

He turned her to face him, suddenly irritated. "I don't want to be your damn job, Katie," he said. "I want to be a lot of things to you, but not a job. And when you are feeling better, we are going to talk." Before she could object, he carried her up the stairs and straight to her room. He set her on the bed, and bent down on one knee in front of her.

"I'm trying to do what is right, Luke," she whispered.

"I know, Katie." He suddenly felt guilty for being so rough on her. "I'm just not sure if I'm capable of letting you do it, under the present setup. I want you too much to keep this just business." His mouth went dry thinking about where they were, but the white line around her mouth that told of pain, plus the dark smudges beneath her eyes, quickly had him checking his desire. "I'll get you that ice."

Luke made fast tracks to the kitchen, lust pumping through him and beating on him with desire. He had to face the facts. He'd told himself he had agreed to this dating facade with Katie because his management had forced his hand. But he'd agreed, because as soon as Katie had walked into his den, he'd wanted her.

His agreement to publicly date her was self-serving, self-rewarding, and he wasn't one for games—didn't appreciate being played, so he didn't do it to other people. He had to make sure Katie knew exactly where he was coming from and where this was going. It was easy to see Katie would find all kinds of reasons to question what was cut-and-dry to him. He wanted her. She wanted him. Hell. Ron had practically shoved them into bed together.

Tossing ice into a plastic bag, he decided he was probably twisting Ron's instructions a bit there, but people dated those they were involved with professionally all the time. Right. Now, if Katie would only see it that way.

His hand tightened on the refrigerator door, an odd sense of not being alone sliding down his spine. Remaining still, he listened but found nothing but silence. He walked to the back-door security panel and checked it. All was intact. He glanced out the window. Nothing but sunlight and flowers. He shook his head, scrubbed his thickening stubble. All this security stuff was making him crazy. Still, he walked to the front door, staying silent, and again checked the security panel, again glanced outside. All was clear.

Shaking off the unease, he redirected his thoughts to Katie and took the stairs two at a time, returning to the guest room. He found Katie lying on her side, her leg stiff and awkward, her eyes shut. He sat down next to her and her eyes opened. "I hate pain medicine," she whispered. "I couldn't seem to make it to the pillow. Can you hand it to me?"

Luke scooted Katie to the top of the bed, taking one

of the pillows and putting it under her knee, propping the ice around it. And then he lay down beside her and pulled her head onto his shoulder. "Rest," he said, and he ran his hand down her hair.

But she already was. Her small hand curled over his heart and her hair sprayed over his chest. Luke swallowed hard, feeling some sort of profound rightness about this that he couldn't begin to understand. He absorbed the moment, Katie sleeping in his arms, a woman who'd stormed into his life like a raging hurricane.

Luke studied the ceiling, not seeing it but seeing himself. He had every reason to be guarded, every reason to hold back with her. He'd been royally screwed over by his ex and by his manager. But he'd always been one to take life on the chin, to make the most of his blessings and not wallow in the negative.

That's why he refused to let the letters and threats steal his focus from the game. Being in the spotlight was part of getting the blessed chance to do what he loved and get paid for it. Shit happened in the spotlight. Shit happened in life.

But after meeting Katie, he was finding some perspective with respect to his behavior in the recent months. He'd become reserved, on guard. And he wasn't going to allow that to happen. No doubt, that left him exposed to manipulation, but every step he'd taken to get where he was today in his life had come with risks. He didn't want to let bad experiences, bad people, change who and what he was. A ballplayer who was grateful for every single opportunity he had in his life, and every person who'd believed in him on the way there. He didn't want to start thinking everyone was out to get him, or get something from him. And he had. He had started feeling that way. No more of that. He wasn't going to stop taking risks. Not on the field and not in his personal life. And he sure wasn't going to miss out on discovering why Katie felt so damn good lying here in his arms.

KATIE FADED in and out of sleep, clinging to the warmth surrounding her. So pleasant. So comfortable. A ringing sound in the distance forced her to leave it behind, her eyes peeling open, bright sunlight piercing her pupils. Her cell phone. Katie sat straight up. Her eyes went wide.

"Luke!" Luke was in bed with her. "Ouch, ouch." Her leg. She reached for it and heard the ringing again. "My phone."

Luke started laughing. "You've managed to panic over me, your leg and your phone in about thirty seconds of being awake. I think you should lie back down and start over."

She forgot her phone and her leg. "You're… We're… Did we?"

He leaned up on his elbows, his T-shirt stretching over his broad chest, muscles flexing beneath the soft material. "I'd like to think you'd remember if we had."

"Good point," she said. So would she? It would be damn near criminal to live out that fantasy and not remember.

"Besides," he said. "I don't take advantage of women while they are drunk or on drugs." He chuckled as if remembering something she could not. "You really weren't kidding about not doing well with pain pills."

No telling what she had said or done when she was

groggy. "Hate them," she said. "Same reason I don't drink. I hate that fuzzy, out-of-focus feeling."

His laughter faded, but the cute dimple in his right cheek did not. "Myself, and most of the hospital staff, gathered that fairly well," he said with playful sarcasm. "Which is why I stayed close—in case you needed anything."

She tilted her head, studied him and his motives. "Close is within hearing range," she said. "Close is not in bed with me."

He didn't seem fazed by her observation. "You were tired and so was I." He dismissed it, as if sleeping in the same bed meant nothing, but they both knew it did. It was intimate. It was…sleeping in the same bed! He glanced at the clock, which read ten-thirty. "We slept about two hours."

Two hours—for two hours Katie had been snuggled close to him, wrapped in those big, strong, wonderful arms, and she didn't remember. That was wrong on so many levels.

"How's your leg?" he asked, snapping her out of her silent regret.

His hair was rumpled and sexy, his eyes full of what appeared to be genuine concern. She didn't answer the question. Instead, she asked one of her own. "You stayed in case I needed anything?"

"Sure. I was worried about you." He sat up, his gaze traveling to the pillow by her leg. "Though I forgot about the ice when I fell asleep." He grabbed the dripping bag that was filled with just water now and carefully placed it on the nightstand by the bed.

Katie had never had a man take care of her like this.

Her parents would have, if they were around. Her sister, yes, before she'd gotten married to her loser husband. Donna would take care of her, if she needed help. But never a man. It felt nice and downright terrifying. She didn't want to feel this, to want this, to rely on someone who wouldn't be there later. If the past few years had taught her anything, it was that.

"We need to switch to heat now anyway," he said, turning back to her, onto his side. Katie quickly tried to wipe away any remnant of emotion as he added. "I've got a heating pad I use on my arm when it gets stiff. You can use that. How often does that leg flare up?"

"Not often really," she told him. "It's unpredictable. Staying active helps, but I have to be careful. I should have been wearing a knee brace and I wasn't. But then, I can be doing absolutely nothing and still aggravate it." She hesitated. "Thank you, Luke."

Their eyes locked, held, the electricity between them instant, intense. "You don't owe me any thanks," he said. "And you didn't answer my question. How is your leg?"

"My calf is throbbing from those damn stitches," she said. "My knee—well—I've learned to live with that during flare-ups. Though the limits it represents—that's harder than anything. It'll calm back down in the next few days."

The air shifted and seconds passed. Seconds laden with sexual tension. Thick with the attraction that had snapped between them from the moment they'd met, the same tension they'd funneled into harsh words and arguments. But there was no argument now. There was only desire. Only need.

"Tell me to go get that heating pad before I don't go at all, Katie," he said, his voice low, gravelly.

Katie's chest tightened, her cheeks heated. She was drowning in the clear promise in his stare. She shut her eyes, tried to block it out. But the instant she looked at him again, the intensity in his gaze pulled her right back in. How had this happened? How had she fallen this much in lust with a man she'd thought she hated only two days before? There were a million reasons to send him away, but suddenly, the lines of right and wrong weren't so black-and-white. Suddenly, there was simply her and Luke. And that felt right; they felt right.

"Stay," she said. "I want you to stay, Luke."

Luke didn't move, didn't blink. "You're sure?" he asked, his voice as intense as his stare. "You want me to stay? Because last night you didn't even want me to kiss you."

"I wanted you to kiss me, Luke. You know I wanted you to kiss me." She reached out and ran her hand through his hair. "And I want you to kiss me now."

He scooted closer, his hand going to her thigh, the calluses of his fingers skimming her bare leg, goose bumps rising in their wake. His lips closed in on hers, but still he held back. "No guilt, Katie. It's like stealing a base—once you commit, you have to own the decision. There are no regrets."

Katie let those words fill her, let them expand with all the possibilities they held: the guilt, the self-doubt, the punishment after the fact that she could manage to dish out to herself—and Lord only knew, she was good at that. But she'd done so much guilt and responsibility these past few years. For the first time in a long time, she didn't feel alone. She didn't want more of that. She wanted Luke. She did. But… "I need to know you understand this changes nothing. I am here to do a job and I plan to do it. I need to know this isn't about you thinking I'll quit the security issue if this happens."

"If I thought for a minute that being with me would distract you from doing your job," he said, "I probably wouldn't want you. It's your strong will and determination that turns me on, Katie. I expect nothing less than you riding my ass about security when we have our clothes back on. Maybe before. But you better damn sure bet I'll likely be complaining about it, too."

Katie found herself smiling inside with those words, because she believed him completely. He would grumble. But she also appreciated his honesty about that fact. He continued, "This here, now—us together—it's about a man and a woman who not only want each other, we have chemistry, Katie. It's not about Ron's agenda or management's or even about a stalker. It's you and me."

He'd said exactly what she both wanted and needed to hear, and Katie allowed herself to let go—to let herself reach for pleasure. She pressed her lips to his, lingered as she absorbed the feel of him, the taste of him. His lips were firm but soft, his restraint evident in the tension of his mouth, his body. He didn't believe she'd committed. "No regrets," Katie whispered, her fingers tracing his jaw as she pulled back to stare at him. "I want this, Luke. I want *you*."

Seconds snapped by, heavy with sexual tension—as if he was somehow silently measuring her commitment—before Luke's hand weaved into her hair, before his lips found hers, his tongue dividing the seam of her lips and plunging into her mouth. Passionate hot kisses followed, his tongue teasing her, pleasing her. She could barely breathe for the rush of need that climbed through her body, expanding within her chest. Her nipples ached and her breasts were heavy. She wanted him to touch her there, wanted to touch him. Her damn leg throbbed and wouldn't move or she would have lifted it over his hip, arched into him. He seemed to sense her need, inching closer, his hand gliding around her scantily clad backside and squeezing.

She moaned into his mouth, slid her hand under his shirt, reveling in the feel of taut, warm skin beneath her palm, the muscles flexing beneath her touch.

"Take this off," she said, shoving the material of his tee upward, her fingers splaying in the springy hair of his chest, nails scraping over his nipples. She could feel the raw need in him building, and it drove her wild. Drove her to demand more. She was going to absorb herself in Luke, keep herself from thinking about doubts, about guilt. She wanted it all—she wanted all of him, and she wanted him naked.

His lips stole away from hers as he maneuvered to take his shirt off. While he did, her hand found his crotch, stroking the hard ridge of his erection. "Katie," he moaned, lying back down. She pressed a hand over those flat, rippling abdominals, and followed with her lips, tracing one muscle after the other, even as her fingers dipped beneath the denim of his pants. Exploring this man's perfect body was exactly the kind of experience and reward she needed.

But suddenly, Luke gently but surely shackled her

hand. "My turn, sweetheart," he said, easing her carefully to her back. "You rest that leg, and let me do all the work." He grabbed the pillow and propped her leg up.

"My leg is fine," she argued.

"And we're going to keep it that way," he said, leaning down and brushing his lips over her knee, easing her good leg wide so that he could slip between the V. He peered up at her, dark lashes veiling eyes laden with a mischievous, sexy promise—the promise of pleasure. Promise of satisfaction.

His lips went back to her sore knee, his tongue flickering seductively against her delicate skin, his hand slowly riding up her thigh as his mouth followed. His teeth and his tongue alternated with delicate, sizzling manipulations until he shoved her shorts up, nipped beneath the hem—licked. Heat pooled low in her stomach, and Katie could feel her core clench with anticipation, her teeth sinking into her bottom lip.

But he kept her waiting, a new pleasure unfolding. He slid that rock-hard body up hers, hands caressing a path beneath her shirt, over her rib cage. Kissed her. Seduced her. Katie faded into a haze of desire that she didn't want to ever leave. And in that haze, somehow her shirt was gone, Luke's hands over her breasts, where her bra had once been, her back arching into his touch. His thumbs stroking her nipples, his tongue gliding along hers with hungry thrusts and deep, passionate demands. She wrapped her free leg around him, arched her hips, wanted more of him, wanted him closer. She could feel the hard length of his erection stretching his jeans, pressing into the center of her body. She wanted it stretching her.

"I want you inside me, Luke," she whispered.

"Soon," he promised, and she realized suddenly she'd said the words out loud.

"Not soon enough," she said hoarsely.

She could feel him smile against her neck. "I don't want to miss one delicious spot." His lips trailed kisses along her skin, causing wicked sensations, until he pressed her breasts together, suckling one nipple and then the other. The points became stiff peaks as he was nipping and biting and then gently licking them, teasing her until she was aching with the need to feel him fill her. Aching to the point that her womb was spasming. He trailed downward, kissing as he went. She trembled with anticipation as he kissed her stomach, when his tongue dipped into her belly button.

Gently, he eased her shorts down her legs, and as aroused as they both were, he was miraculously, amazingly careful of her injuries. He tossed the shorts aside, his hand sliding up her uninjured calf and thigh, and before she knew his intention, Luke lifted her leg over his shoulder. Suddenly, his tongue lapped at her clit, then closed down on it. Katie gasped as he drew her deep into his mouth, his tongue sliding along her sensitive flesh, two of his fingers entering her, stroking her. Katie's hands dug into the blanket, her hips rocking against his mouth, his fingers.

"Luke," she panted, her breath hitching, stealing her thoughts, or maybe that was his breath, intimately warming her. She tried again. "I…" *want you inside me.* But she couldn't say it. She couldn't say anything. She could only *feel*. She could only need. Her fingers stretched, reaching for his head, even as his fingers stretched inside her, taking her further into that place of no return. But, damn it, she wanted to push him away and make him undress, to feel his body above her, around her. At the same time, her body was making a desperate appeal for him to continue, humming in response to the sinful play of his mouth, tongue and fingers.

In some distant place she heard her own moans, her own breathing. She tried to hold his head exactly where he was, all thought of stopping him gone, but she couldn't quite touch him. Not with her leg up over his shoulder. She lifted her hips farther. She wanted her other leg up there, too, but it was stiff; it wouldn't move.

Her head twisted from side to side, her hand molding her breasts, pinching her nipples. The other resorted to the blanket again, curling her fingers in the cloth as tension coiled in her core. Tighter, tighter. Every muscle in her body tensed, and then it happened. The spasms exploded low in her belly, and then it was as if a gate opened and a flood of pleasure washed over her—her body clenched around his fingers, her breath exploded from her lungs in a gasp. And then another. Luke rocked his mouth and fingers with her, lapped at her with his tongue, fast and then slower, and slower, until he brought her down, eased her to completion.

Katie collapsed with the final moment of release, every bit of energy she possessed gone. Every ounce of her sated, satisfied in a way that consumed her as much as the pleasure had. Luke carefully put her leg down, then kissed her stomach. Her fingers went to his hair as he stared up at her, his eyes tender rather than demanding.

"Luke, that was… I am—"

"Luke! Katie!" It was Ron's voice, and all that sated, wonderful, amazing pleasure was gone.

"Oh, no!" Kate whispered, trying to sit up.

"How the hell did Ron get into my house?" Luke murmured. "Unless Maria showed up and let him in." His hand settled on her shoulder. "Easy. Don't hurt your leg."

"The door!" she whispered fiercely, holding herself up on her hands. "Luke, I'm naked here. Please. Shut the door."

"Easy, sweetheart," he said. "Everything is going to be fine." He slid off the bed and shut the door, locking it, as well.

It was not fine, she thought, nor was it going to be fine. In a matter of hours, she'd gone from a professional who'd landed a job that would get her sister out of hot water, to being injured, drugged, seduced and now humiliated.

Door secure, Luke scrubbed his heavily shadowed jaw and snagged his shirt, slipping it over his head. Katie scrambled for her clothes. Luke found her shorts on the floor and handed them to her.

She struggled to find her shirt, frustrated when she couldn't move well enough to find anything, which only served to remind her that her crazy libido had landed her in this hot water. She threw her hands in the air. "Where did you put my bra?"

Luke arched a brow. "Where did *I* put your bra?" he challenged. "I seem to remember you were involved in disposing of it, as well." He scooped up her bra and shirt and tossed them at her, frustration in the hard set of his jaw.

Katie glared at him, catching her things, wishing like hell he wasn't watching her as she attempted to get the bra over her arms. The act of putting on the damn undergarment made her feel somehow far more exposed than when he'd taken it off, and she couldn't get it hooked.

Suddenly, Luke was sitting beside her. "Let me help."

"No, I—" Her words lodged in her throat as he turned her and hooked her bra. It was such a small thing, but so large—an act of intimacy a couple would share. They weren't a couple. He was a job. She should have remembered that.

Luke offered her shirt to her, and she fumbled around and managed to get it on. Immediately, she started for the edge of the bed. She didn't look at Luke. She couldn't deal with him now. First, she had to deal with Ron.

"You did nothing wrong," Luke said softly. "*We* did nothing wrong. If Ron says otherwise, I'll damn sure tell him so, too."

"No. Please don't. You've done enough. Just let me handle it."

Luke was on his feet in an instant, facing her. "You're obviously upset, so I'm not going to take that remark like the slap it felt like." He stared at her, his gaze fixed, steady, assessing. He read through her tension. He knew what she was feeling. And his words proved it. "No regrets. That was the agreement."

"That was before Ron showed up while we were in

bed together," she spouted back tightly. "That wasn't in the plan." Not that she'd had a plan. That was clear.

"We are not children caught by Dad," he said. "We're consenting adults."

He had nothing to lose here. But she had a reputation and a way to pay her sister's debt off. "I'm here to work, Luke. Not become one of your groupies."

"Is that what you think this is?" he demanded. "Me turning you into some sort of groupie?"

That was when Ron's voice sounded from the hall-way. "Katie! Luke!"

Luke ground his teeth. "The man needs to learn to knock at the door," he grumbled irritably as he stalked toward the door.

7

THE RUMBLING of male voices disappeared down the stairs, and Katie slipped on her sneakers, which she assumed Luke must have taken off. She struggled to stand, putting all her weight on her good leg. Dumb knee, not to mention her calf. It hurt worse from having a needle poked through it than it did from the cut. Katie dug her cell phone out of her purse and checked caller ID. Donna had called. Not once, but several times, which meant she had something important to share. But first she had to deal with the current situation.

Katie headed to the hallway, hesitating as she shoved a hand through her messy hair and then over her rumpled clothes. She prayed she looked as if she'd spent hours in the E.R., with no telltale signs that hours in bed with Luke had followed.

She clutched the winding wooden rail of the stairwell and sucked up the pain, ready to get this over with. When she finally managed to reach floor level, Katie followed the echo of voices and found Luke and Ron standing in the kitchen.

Or what was left of it.

"Good grief," Katie said, pressing a hand to her fore-head, appalled at the sight of broken glass, smashed pictures and food products dumped everywhere. "What happened?"

Both men were staring at her; both seemed to be filled with condemnation. Luke, because she'd said she felt like a groupie. Ron, because he thought she was one, given the scene in front of them. The attention from both wasn't easy to bear, considering her body still hummed from Luke's touch. Her cheeks were probably flushed. Her lips swollen.

Ron cast Katie a suspicious look, and spoke with a deliberateness in his tone that said she was right—she looked as if she'd just had a sexcapade with his client. "You tell me," he said. "I arrived here to find the door cracked. I came in and found it like this."

Katie grimaced at the obvious implication that she had been doing something other than her job, the heat of arousal quickly becoming the heat of anger. She and Ron obviously needed to have a talk in private.

She forced inner calm and focused on her job. "Was there any sign of forced entry at all?"

"None," Ron assured her. "But we checked the security panels. They're turned off."

Luke quickly explained, "When I came downstairs to get ice earlier, I had this weird vibe, like I wasn't alone, so I checked those panels and they were on."

Katie frowned, trying to make sense of this in her head. "We've only been back from the E.R. a few hours." Realization washed over her at the same moment her eyes collided with Luke's, a silent understanding between them that neither of them dared to reveal to Ron.

The kitchen had been destroyed while they were in that bed together. Katie's hand went to her throat. The bedroom door had been open. Whoever had been here might well have watched them together.

A Spanish exclamation pierced the air as Maria appeared beside Katie, taking in the mess. She charged forward, Jessica right behind her. Jessica brushed past Katie, a distinct chill frosting up the air as she knocked into Katie's arm.

"I called Maria to clean up," Ron supplied, glancing between Luke and Katie.

Katie looked at Luke. "I take it that means we aren't calling the police?" A challenge laced her voice. The police could fingerprint.

"No police," Luke said firmly. "The odds that they will find anything aren't worth the odds something will slip out to the press. I don't need that kind of crap right before my season starts."

Her eyes locked with his. "We'll keep it out of the papers."

"No," he said, his jaw tense. "No police."

"I have to agree," Ron said, his tone as starched as his white shirt. "The last thing we need right now is management getting word of more trouble after I've promised them this is handled." His lips thinned with disapproval, his gaze raking Katie. "Clearly it was not."

Katie drew her spine stiff, irritated at the obvious jab. Yes, she'd been in bed with Luke. No, that wasn't professional, and it should not be repeated, but she was downright offended by Ron's inference that her failure had led to the kitchen vandalism.

Katie glanced toward the sink where Jessica was running water, her back to the group. Then she flashed a look at Ron and Luke and motioned them to the other room, aware she could not talk in front of Maria and Jessica without blowing her cover. The three of them gathered in the office as they had before.

The instant the door was shut, Katie whirled on Ron. "I get that you don't want to look bad to management," she said grumpily, "but I've been here less than forty-eight hours, without so much as a proper file to study."

"You have a file," Ron countered.

"Twelve hours ago before I left for a gala you knew about for months and didn't bother to tell me about," she snapped. "When my team is here, and I have the proper data to do my job, then you can blame me for failures. Not until then." She leaned against the door, her knee killing her, an irritation she didn't have time for when she had so many others. "I'm not even sure what happened here today was related to the letters."

"What are you saying?" Ron demanded, his arms crossed in front of his body.

"Jessica," she said. "She's jealous. She's young. She has the codes to get inside the house."

"No way," Luke said, leaning against the desk, his arms flexing beneath his shirt, drawing Katie's unintentional inspection. She swallowed hard, blaming the pain medication for her lack of focus, as he added, "She's a good kid. She wouldn't do something like this."

"A kid," Katie pointedly repeated. "Emotional,

jealous and upset about my appearance here, Luke. It makes sense."

He made a frustrated sound. "The next thing you know, you'll have her cutting and pasting letters."

Katie hesitated, unwilling to rule out anything. She couldn't shake the idea that Jessica had come into the house, seen her and Luke together, and lashed out by destroying the kitchen. But believing that Jessica had been obsessing about Luke enough to have written those letters was treading through deeper waters.

"I think we need to look at all options," she said. "We certainly need to know if Jessica has been in any trouble. I'll have my people look into it. I doubt that's something Maria would announce to her employer, no matter how close you are to her, Luke." As far as Katie was concerned, they couldn't get those letters to the FBI lab soon enough. "I'm assuming you changed the locks and codes after the issues with your ex?" she asked.

His expression darkened. "Months ago."

"I figured as much," she said. "But we'll have to change the locks and the codes again today. Once my guys get here, they'll analyze the entire security system and make needed changes. But no one gets the new codes without my approval."

Luke pushed off the desk, ran a hand through his hair in frustration. "I'll give Maria a month off with pay. I hope like hell that's enough time to make this go away."

Katie's cell phone rang, and she glanced at the number. Donna again. Her heart hammered in her chest. She'd called so many times, Katie was starting to feel nervous. What if something was wrong with her sister?

"I need to take this, but, Luke, don't give Maria time off. Not until we have time to think it through. If Jessica is the culprit, we don't need to send her warning signs. We need to catch her in action." Her phone kept ringing. "I really need to take this." She flipped open her phone and answered as she made a hobbling escape. "Hello."

"The point in having a phone," Donna said immediately, "is to answer it."

"What's going on?" Katie asked urgently. She slipped into the den where she could grab some privacy, rather than climbing the stairs.

"Noah and Josh are on their way to you this afternoon," she said. "They finally wrapped things up here. They get into the airport at eleven-fifteen."

Having considered moving Luke away to a hotel that night, until she had the place secure—something she'd known he wouldn't be pleased about—Katie absorbed that news with relief.

A few minutes later, Katie ended the call, relieved that her sister was safe, and that Noah and Josh would arrive soon. She'd also asked Donna to run checks on both Jessica and Maria. Donna had the electronic file Ron had provided, as well, and was working though it with a fine-tooth comb.

Ready for a shower and some inner perspective, Katie headed to the door only to be cut off by Ron, who now stood in the doorway.

"I only have one question," he said.

Her chest tight, she answered cautiously. "All right."

"We've established that you and Luke playing at dating works in theory. It keeps the press off his back, and

keeps the team from panicking about a potential threat.
But I need to know right now—is this thing with you
and Luke a problem?"

Thing. She assumed that was his code word for *sex*.
She inhaled sharply despite having expected this question. It wasn't an unfair question, after all. He'd hired
her to do a job, full stop. "There is no problem, Ron."
Because Katie wasn't going to let there be a problem.
She had the *thing* with Luke, whatever it was, within
her grasp.

He gave her a curt nod, surprising her by disappearing through the doorway without another word. Katie let
out a breath of relief, thankful he'd let it go that easily.

And with Noah and Josh showing up shortly, she and
Luke would have proper established boundaries. Now,
she simply needed to come to a workable understanding
with him. Then control would be restored, and she and
her team would make this stalker problem go away for
Luke.

Unbidden, a very female part of her flared to life and
cursed the fact that she and Luke had been interrupted
before they'd completed their *thing*. Control would be
so much easier if she didn't have the memory of how
good *almost* making love to Luke Winter had been.

NEAR EIGHT in the evening, hours after the meeting with
Ron, Katie sat alone at the informal dining table at the
back of Luke's kitchen, the house to herself. Ron had
taken Luke to ball practice, and Katie had stayed behind
to deal with the locksmith and the kitchen cleanup. She
didn't like Luke being out without her, but Ron was with

him, and they had all agreed, she could only follow Luke around so much without breaking her cover.

After what had felt like chaos for most of the day, finally, the house was empty. Katie sat with her much-improved leg—thanks to several painkillers—propped up on a chair, her notebook computer open in front of her. Soon enough, though, Luke would return, and it would be only the two of them—alone again—a host of sexual tension bursting with life, and she didn't know what to do about it.

Sadly, she saw Noah's and Josh's appearance later that night as a way to keep her chemistry with Luke from eroding her common sense. A buffer was good. The memories of what they'd done in that bedroom—the kisses, the touches, the pleasure—were diminishing her ability to think straight. And when Ron had surprised them, she'd felt guilty, she'd felt wrong.

But now...now, she felt conflicted. She wanted Luke safe. She wanted Luke in bed. She wanted to do what was right. Could all of these things happen together? She wasn't sure, and since she had no time to really evaluate things objectively, she had to focus on what had happened today, and on Luke's protection.

Beside her, Katie's cell phone rang. No caller ID. Katie tensed. It could be Luke. It could be Ron. She answered. Silence filled the line. "Hello?" More silence. Her gut clenched. Not again. "You'll get your money!"

She hung up and dialed her sister. No answer. Carrie never answered her calls. She was angry at Katie. As if Katie were the cause of everything bad in her life. Losing her parents. Marrying a creep of a man. And it hurt. Katie felt like she had lost Carrie, too. "Carrie," she said into the voice mail. "Please call me back. Let me know you're okay. I love you, sis."

Katie tried to refocus on her research, but in the back of her mind she worried. Maybe she'd been too hard on Carrie over this gambling thing. It must be hard to have a husband who treated her like a rug, on top of the loss of their parents.

She shook off the thought. She couldn't let the guilt eat her alive. This job was paying off the gambling debt, which was a monster. Donna was watching over Carrie. Everything was okay.

Katie punched her e-mail and found one from Donna—an Excel spreadsheet of Luke's team that included everything from their date of signing and contract terms, to their marital status, even spousal names. Donna was using that list to add any red flags that her research had dug up on the different players. Katie planned to go down the list of friends and family with Luke, a process she was quite certain he would not be thrilled about, especially after seeing his reaction to Jessica's potential guilt.

Katie's mind went back to Carrie, back to that second silent phone call. She dialed Donna. "Is everything okay there? Carrie is fine?"

"Sugar," she said. "Everything is peachy. I went by her place this morning. Well…aside from the fact that her loser husband was there, everything was peachy. I think Carrie is coming around. We had a chat about leaving her loser husband."

Katie perked up. "You did?"

"Yep," she said. "Even got her to agree to meet that new attorney who opened an office down the hall from us."

"I don't believe it," Katie said. "Finally she's going to leave him."

"Nothing is for sure," Donna warned, "and frankly, it's best you don't say a word to her about this. She seems to do everything you tell her not to do and vice versa."

Katie rested her elbows on the table. "Isn't that the truth?"

"Too bad she needs that attorney for a divorce," Donna said. "He's a cutie pie, that one."

"I'm surprised you aren't happy she needs him for the divorce," Katie said laughingly. "That makes him open season for you."

"It goes against my better judgment to date someone I have to see every day."

Katie snorted. "That's called marriage."

"Which is not on my agenda. So thanks, but no, thanks," she said. "Speaking of men, how's Luke doing?"

Katie frowned, determined to avoid the personal place this was going. No way was she admitting that not only had Luke taken her to the E.R. and tended her injury, he'd tended to her pleasure, too. If she didn't admit it had happened, it hadn't. Right? Right. That was her strategy, and she was sticking to it.

"Actually," Katie said. "I just forwarded you an e-mail from Ron with the team roster. We need to run background checks on everyone and look for secondary links to Luke." She thought back to the party. "Also— there was an agent I met here. I'll e-mail you his info. He was trying to grab Luke's attention."

"Aren't they all? The man is a hot commodity."

"Regardless, it might be worth checking out. He showed up at a charity event that Luke was attending when Ron didn't feel the need to be there. I'm wondering if it wasn't specifically to court Luke. Perhaps he wants to be the hero who rebuilds Luke's career once it tanks."

"Nothing is going to tank Luke's career," Donna assured her, "as long as he pitches well and stays out of any self-induced trouble, like drugs and alcohol."

"Luke is convinced he's going to have a great season," Katie said. "And it's early, but so far, he appears to be pretty squeaky clean. He doesn't even have beer in his fridge. Just a fetish for protein shakes and, apparently, ice cream." Blizzards. He'd talked about ice-cream treats as she would talk about chocolate. It was cute, endearing even. She liked Luke. Why did she have to like him, damn it? She finished up her talk with Donna and forwarded the e-mails.

With a sigh, Katie tossed a pen on the table; she'd been scribbling some notes as she scanned the Internet. Her drinking glass was empty, and she did a slow stroll to the kitchen, her calf far more painful than her knee, which was a huge relief. It meant she didn't have a serious flare-up to contend with.

She was refilling her glass with iced tea when the front door opened and closed. Katie turned to find Luke standing in the kitchen doorway, the picture of country boy sex appeal—his light brown hair rumpled, as if the wind or his fingers had gotten a hold of it.

Her mouth went dry; her nipples tightened against her thin bra. She abandoned the glass and crossed her arms in front of her chest, afraid he'd notice her obvious reaction. No matter how much she wanted to stick to strictly business with Luke, her body wasn't cooperating. And no matter how hard she tried to keep her eyes level with his, she did a full-out inspection of his faded jeans and the light blue T-shirt that fit his chest like artwork rather than cotton. To complete his look, there were the scuffed boots that somehow made the entire look ten times more sexy. It was clear—you could take Luke out of Texas, but you couldn't take the Texas heat out of Luke.

"I see you got past the new security panel okay," she said, having called Luke on his cell phone and left a message with the keypad entrance code.

He sauntered forward, leaning on the kitchen island, facing her, close to her. So close. Wonderfully close. Sinfully close. She had to get away.

"Worked fine," he said, glancing around the kitchen. "Looks like there was no permanent damage here."

"You lost some dishes and plates," she said, following his lead. They were making small talk. Avoiding what was between them, or perhaps working toward it. Avoiding was better. Not forever, but tonight.

Thunder rolled outside the window, shaking the glass door, almost as if Mother Nature knew her thoughts and objected to her strategy.

"Your crew is going to get a bumpy plane ride in," Luke commented.

She stared at his chest. It seemed a good plan—not looking into those all-too-knowing eyes. Instead, she found herself admiring the damn blue T-shirt again, and worse, mentally visualizing how glorious he'd been without it, how wonderful that smooth, taut skin had felt beneath her hands.

She jerked her gaze upward. "They're taking a taxi when they arrive so it won't matter what time they get in."

"They are due in at eleven-fifteen, so with delays and the taxi, they'll arrive after midnight, I suspect," he said, the unspoken implication there—they were alone for a while.

She wanted to be alone with him. She shouldn't want to be alone with him. Her chin lifted, those ice-gray eyes of his anything *but* icy—they were heat, fire, seduction. The room seemed to shrink, and with it, her hands-off resolve. Desperately, she reached for it again, somehow found a calm, businesslike tone. "I talked with Ron on the phone, just a bit ago. We've decided to say Noah and Josh are my brothers, here visiting a few days. We don't want to set off any alarms for the team or your stalker. And we have to think about Maria and Jessica."

"Why would your brothers be at my house?"

"I'm a professional dancer who travels as much as you do," she said. "That'll check out if anyone looks it up. I've done plenty of tours. I'm taking some time off, traveling with you. My brothers wanted to see me before I hit the road again. It also makes us look close, like we've been dating awhile, off everyone's radar. We'll need to practice our stories and get them down perfectly."

"You really think you and your team can end this before Texas, like you told Ron?"

"I'm hopeful, yes," she confirmed. "But we'll evaluate the situation quickly once my team arrives, and if we feel the situation will extend to Texas, conversations about travel will need to take place. I'll want you close to me where I can best protect you."

Their eyes held, awareness between them, the possibility of shared hotel rooms a reminder of an intimate encounter unfinished. Was she insane to think she could keep her distance from Luke?

"How's your leg?" he asked, clearly ready to put the security issues aside.

"It's fine. Better." She could barely breathe. When in her life had a man ever stolen her breath simply by looking at her? Never. Never was how many times. She cleared her throat and motioned toward the table where she'd been working. "I have a list of questions," she managed to say, her voice somewhat steady when she felt far from it. "Maybe you could answer them for me?"

He didn't move. Neither did she. She didn't want to move anywhere but toward him. Yet she had to put distance between them.

Finally, he said, "Is this how it's going to be, Katie?" he asked. "We act as if nothing happened between us? As if we both don't want to go back upstairs and finish what we started?"

Going back upstairs and finishing what they started sounded far too good. Katie found herself squeezing her legs together at the suggestion. Somehow, she kept an impassive expression.

Unfortunately, she also put her foot right in her big mouth. "I'm trying to do my job, Luke," she managed. The minute she said those words, she knew she'd made a mistake.

His mood shifted, turned darker; it radiated off him, as stormy as the weather outside. "Your job," he said flatly. Suddenly, he moved, closing the distance between them, his hands pressing into the counter on either side of her. He didn't touch her, but his body aligned with hers, the heat radiating off him, into her. "Is that what we are back to? I'm your job?"

"Luke," she said, her voice not even sounding like her own. *Don't touch him. Don't do it.* Her hands itched to flatten themselves on his chest. "I *am* here for a job. To find out who your stalker is."

"And you think pretending not to want me while pretending to date me is what's right? You think that makes logical sense?" When he put it that way, no. No, it did not make sense. He pressed onward, his voice full of confessions that reached beyond his words. "I want you, Katie. I can't stop thinking about your soft moans and your silky skin." He stared at her, waited for her to react.

Seconds from caving in to her desire for him, from reaching for Luke, Katie struggled to keep up her resistance. Luke watched her, his face filling with dissatisfaction.

With a frustrated sound, he pushed off the counter. "If this is how you want it, if you want to pretend in public and pretend in private, then so be it. We'll pretend. But be honest about what's really going on, Katie. Being with me isn't keeping you from doing your job. We talked about that. We came to an agreement. You're hiding behind your job as an excuse to hide from whatever is going on in that head of yours. You're running, and I don't think it's from me. I think it's from yourself."

Her heart raced with his assessment, the same one Donna had made. "I'm not running. I'm not making an excuse. I'm taking a step back, in light of today's events, and evaluating my actions."

"Evaluating?" he challenged. "You know what. You just keep evaluating. Evaluate your little heart out. I'm going to bed." He started to turn, stopped. Dropped his bombshell. "We have to be at the coach's house tomorrow for a season kickoff barbecue."

"Barbecue?"

"Right. Wives. Girlfriends. Family. I've never brought anyone with me before. So, we're going to need to do some really fine pretending, Katie. Of course, we could just say we're having our first fight. That won't require much pretending." He was pissed. Pissed and frustrated. She could see it all over his face. "Two o'clock. Be ready." He turned away, began to move toward the hall.

Katie's racing heart shuddered momentarily to a halt, before her mind splintered into a million pieces—a million thoughts. Luke was right. Her job was an excuse. She was afraid of losing herself again in a man and his career, afraid that she would cease to exist if she and Luke began to become a couple. But she wasn't the same person she'd been when that had happened to her before; she wasn't.

"Luke!" she called out, stopping him in his tracks. He faced her, waited with an expectant look on his too-handsome face. "I don't want to go to that barbecue having a fight, and I don't want to pretend I don't want you. I do want you."

He didn't immediately respond. "I like you, Katie, all of you, just as you are, but I won't do this back-and-forth again. You're either in the game or you're out."

She didn't need to think about that. Not anymore. "I'm in on one condition."

"I'm not really into conditions right now," he said, his lips a hard line.

She walked toward him. "I think you'll like this condition." She pressed her hand to his chest. Warmth radiated up her arm, butterflies fluttering in her stomach.

"I'm listening."

"Since we had our first fight," she said, drawing the words out, "shouldn't we have makeup sex?"

A slow smile lifted the corners of his tempting mouth a second before he reached for her. And suddenly, wonderfully, they were crazy-hot kissing, and Katie had a good idea they weren't going to make it to the bedroom. At least not for round one.

8

SHE TASTED of iced tea laced with a ray of sunshine, and was the only good thing that had come from this stalker who'd now managed to invade his life. And as much as he'd tried to convince himself he wasn't rattled, the kitchen incident had rattled him. The fact that he couldn't go to practice without an escort also rattled him. The fact that he couldn't pretend to be unaffected, at least not to himself, scared the shit out of him.

He didn't want to be scared; he didn't want the potential nightmare that being scared could bring to his game, exactly why he'd resisted, even denied, that he had a stalker. Because once he accepted that fact, then it was in his head, and it would be even when he stepped on the mound. And pitching was what he did. It was his life. Without it, he didn't know who he was.

And so he drank of that sunshine that was Katie. Drank her in to forget the threats, forget the upset. Katie didn't want him for his career. And right now, more than ever, that felt right, it felt perfect.

He deepened the kiss, drank of her more completely. She whimpered into his mouth, and he felt the sound as readily as he heard it, felt it in the jolt of lust it shot through his limbs, straight to his groin. Felt it in the comfort that she was no longer anywhere near trying to escape, or redrawing some imaginary line between them and claiming it protected them both. He didn't want to be protected; he wanted to be absorbed, lost inside her.

A wild rush of need expanded inside him and he reached deep to slow down, fearful he would injure Katie's knee. He gently lifted her on top of the low counter, thankful for the design that put her hips even with his. The instant she was stably positioned, he eased between her thighs, inside the V of her body, his mouth slanting over hers. He could almost feel the heat rushing off her, anticipating the instant he would feel all that heat wrapped around him, stroking his cock. And her kisses—hot, hungry kisses that said, once she'd decided she wanted this, she wanted him completely.

His hands traveled her rib cage, her breasts. Katie arched into the touch, her palms tracing his biceps and shoulders. "I need you inside me," she whispered against his lips. The boldness of those words drove into him, hammered him with desire.

Luke tugged her shirt over her head, tossed it aside. She wore a sexy sheer white bra that outlined pink, pebbled nipples. He all but groaned at the sight as he lowered his head and covered one stiff peak with his mouth. She leaned back, one palm on the counter behind her, holding her weight upright, the other in his hair. She was panting, the scent of her arousal ripping through his senses. He reached up and shoved down the lace covering her breast, suckled the nipple gently, then nipped with his teeth. She cried out his name.

"Take this off," he said, fingering her bra and then leaning back to rip his shirt over his head.

A second later, he ran his arms up her back and pressed her naked breasts against his chest, kissing her neck, her lips, her neck again. She was so sweet, he wanted all of her now, yet he wanted this to last. It was a conflicted, hot, wild feeling.

His hand slid between her legs, the wet heat radiating through her shorts. Hunger rolled through him. He tossed her shorts and then found her waistband. He didn't have to tell her what to do, either. She was as ready as he was. Katie lifted her hips as he pulled at the material, panties and all.

Luke spread Katie wide again, but he didn't give in to the need to fill her. Instead, he looked at her. "Beautiful," he said, running his hands up slender, sleekly muscled thighs, until his thumbs stroked the glistening liquid of her arousal.

"Luke," she gasped. "Stop teasing me."

He slipped a finger inside her, then two, exploring her body, her pleasure. Leaning forward and suckling one of her nipples into his mouth. She moaned, her arm wrapping around his shoulder, her hips rocking against the motion of his fingers.

He used his free hand to squeeze her other breast. He wasn't gentle, either—it was clear she didn't want gentle by the desperateness of her rocking against his hand. She wanted fast and hard. He wanted whatever pleased her—he wanted her to come, to milk his fingers the way she was going to milk his cock. And she did just that and more—oh, yeah, she did. Rocking into the caresses of his hand and fingers, moaning into his mouth. She clung to his shoulders until she shattered around him.

"That's it, baby," he murmured near her ear, nipping her delicate lobe and kissing her neck. Leading her to completion, before he finally could wait no more. He unzipped his pants, freeing his throbbing erection and shoving his pants and underwear to his ankles, somehow managing to snag a condom from his wallet without much delay, but he didn't put it on. Not yet. Soon.

He gripped the width of his cock, brought it to the damp heat of her core, to the temptation to slide right in and forget the condom. Knew he had to sheathe himself now, before he didn't do it at all. It would be so easy to slide inside her, to feel that warm, wonderful heat. He brought the plastic wrapper to his mouth to tear it open.

Katie grabbed it. "Let me." She brought the package to *her* teeth, ripped it open as he had planned to, her eyes holding his as she did, a seductive message in their depths. His cock thickened with the intended imagery, the idea of her mouth on his body.

Thankfully, within seconds she was touching him, fingers exploring his erection, before rolling the condom down his length. As soon as it was in place, he brought the head of his cock to her glistening feminine lips. Teased them both as he caressed her there, then barely dipped his head inside her. His breath lodged in his chest at the feel of her, and all resolve to go slowly slipped away.

He thrust into her and she clung to him, tightening her arms around his neck. It quickly became clear that the counter was not going to allow him to get deep enough; he wanted deep, he wanted more, all of her. And she knew it, too. She all but climbed on top of him just as he palmed her lush backside and picked her up, pushing her against his cock. He used his legs and his hips to thrust as hard as he could. Now her full breasts were pressed to his chest, her face buried in his neck. Still, he wanted more, needed more. He not only had to have this woman, he *felt her,* in a way he'd never felt another woman, on a level that went beyond the physical. And by the time her orgasm shuddered around him, stealing his breath and his release in the same second, he knew he hadn't had his fill of Katie. Not anywhere near it.

KATIE STARTED laughing as Luke sat her back down on the counter. "You never even took your pants off," she pointed out. "What if you would have tripped?"

"I wouldn't have fallen," he said, laughing as he disposed of the condom in the wastebasket and then pulled his pants back up. "And even if I had—I was feeling no pain, I can promise you that."

He closed the distance between them, pleased when she held his face and kissed him sweetly. His hands slid over her slender rib cage, grazing the gentle curves of her bare breasts. He felt her shiver. "So," he said softly, loving how easily she responded to his touch. "Have we successfully made up, Katie?"

"No," she said, mischief sparking in her eyes. "I don't think we have. I think we need to try again. I'm willing if you are."

A return smile tugged at his lips. "How willing, I

wonder?" he challenged, making no effort to hide the rough edge of desire coloring his tone.

"What did you have in mind?" she asked playfully.

His fingers brushed her bottom lip before his tongue followed. "I want it all this time, Katie. No inhibitions. No holding back." For reasons he couldn't begin to explain, he wanted that full commitment from her. That decision to fully be with him. Up until now, he didn't believe he'd gotten that from her.

She pulled away, hands on his shoulders, surprise on her face. "You think I was holding back? Because I have to tell you, I didn't feel like I was holding back." She'd felt wild, and yes, willing.

"What we just had was good, damn good, but that was frenzied make-up sex, after a tug-of-war over whether we'll be together or not. This time there is no frenzied rush, Katie. This time is slow and thoughtful. No wondering if what happens is the heat of the moment rather than our choice, our decision together. This time we're making love, not having sex." A flutter in her stomach erupted with heat spreading through her limbs. Make love. She wanted that. But she was scared of being vulnerable, of getting hurt again.

Letting loose a nervous bubble of laughter, she whispered, "I do believe this was my first spontaneous eruption of lust. I liked it."

He didn't laugh. His eyes darkened, his hand sliding up her back, erotic with gentle demand. "Say it," he ordered, intensity suddenly crackling from him.

"Say what?" She blinked.

"Say…'Luke, I want you to make love to me.'"

Her lashes lowered, her heart lodged in her throat as a moment of fight or flight took hold.

"Katie," he whispered, his hand framing her face, bringing her gaze to his. "I need to know you meant what you said when you stopped me from walking away. That we are really in this together." There was a rawness to his tone, honesty and real emotion in his eyes, a hitch to his voice as he added, "Because if we aren't—"

She pressed her lips to his. "Make love to me," she said softly into his mouth. "We're in this together, Luke. We are."

He didn't give her time to change her mind. Luke wrapped his arms around her back and cradled her, carrying her toward the den, not upstairs. And she was glad for it—she didn't want to wait. She wanted him now. Soon. Not soon enough.

He stopped at the light switch as they entered, kissing her even as he reached and turned the dial, casting a dim, sexy glow over the room.

Staring down at her, he confessed, "You have no idea how much I want you."

Katie inhaled a deep breath, absorbing both his words and his spicy male scent, then nuzzled his neck. He felt good, he felt right. She didn't want to be scared. She didn't want to think about the reasons this might be a mistake.

And when he settled her on the soft leather couch and shoved aside the coffee table, she shoved aside any such thoughts, enthralled by the sight of him undressing.

She curled her legs to her chest, wrapped her arms around her knees and watched his every move. And he let her. Oh, yes, he stared at her with such heat and desire in his eyes that she knew this was going to be a delicious escape. An escape she wanted. With him.

HE WAS gorgeous. Katie watched as Luke stripped down to nothing, her mouth dry and her stomach swirling with heat. Her thighs ached, her core wet with the need to feel him inside her again. She didn't know where to start in her admiration. There were so many joys to this man's body, and she allowed herself to luxuriate in all of them. His chest and shoulders were broad, defined, pecs sprinkled with the perfect amount of springy, light brown hair. His legs powerful, his abdominals damn near a work of art, valleys dipping around hard muscles. She wanted to kiss a path around every single one of them, too.

Her gaze lowered, a soft moan all but escaping her lips. His cock jutted forward, long and hard, promising more pleasure. It thickened under her inspection, darkened. If she could have crawled on her knees and fallen beneath it, licked the glistening pebble of liquid on the tip, she would have.

Her gaze went to his. "No holding back," he said softly. "Put your legs down, Katie."

She swallowed, realizing he wasn't moving. He was standing there, watching her as she was him. Which seemed a fair enough trade. Slowly, she lowered her legs, pressed her hands to the couch, her breasts exposed to his hungry stare that traveled lower.

He went down on his knees in front of her but didn't touch her. "Open for me, baby," he ordered softly.

That he wasn't touching her somehow made the order more erotic. Slowly, she did as he said. Inched her thighs apart, spread her legs for him. His eyes seemed to caress and touch every inch of her.

"Beautiful," he said hoarsely, arousal lancing the one word that pulsed through her like a vibration. Heat spread through her limbs, expanding within her chest, set her heart to racing. She was panting. Panting and the man was not even touching her. Nor she him. It was as if he'd settled a barrier between them, an erotically charged barrier that only he could break. She'd never experienced anything like it in her life.

"Luke," she said, all but pleading. "Please."

His gaze riveted upward to meet hers. "Please what, Katie?"

"Touch me."

"Where?" he asked.

"Anywhere," she said.

"Show me where. Show me how."

Vulnerability assailed her. "Luke," she pleaded again. The truth was, she'd never touched herself for a man. Never even considered it. Certainly, she knew her body, felt comfortable in her own skin. She had been a dancer, her craft being an extension of sensuality to some degree. But touching herself for a man had always felt like giving away a piece of herself reserved for her and her alone.

"I won't take you anyplace you don't want to go, Katie," he promised, his eyes holding hers, the air charged with sexual energy. "Anywhere you touch, I'll touch."

She swallowed against the sudden dryness in her throat. Could she touch herself in front of him? She'd never done that with a man. Never felt comfortable enough, free enough. He'd touch where she touched, he said. And she wanted him to touch her. Wanted it far more than she wanted control, she realized with shock. Luke felt safe. Luke whom she'd tried so hard to demonize, to make the enemy. It was insanity.

She reached up and touched her breasts, filled her hands with them, pinched her nipples. Watched him watching her. Felt her womb clench at the intense look on his face. Her fingers twirled her nipples. She moaned softly. "You like it when I do this?"

"I do," he said. "But you're going to like it even more when I do it." His voice lowered. "Show me where to touch you, Katie. Show me where to taste you."

Taste. Those lips. That tongue. She'd already experienced the pleasures they represented, and she didn't need any more encouragement. Her hands began to travel, over her neck, back over her breasts, pressing them together, her nipples peeking through her fingers.

Luke leaned forward and ran his tongue over them, one peak and then the next. Lick, swirl, lick.

Her hands went to his hair. His name whispered from her lips. "Luke."

More licking, a delicate scrape of teeth, and then he leaned back. "Show me more, Katie. Where do you need me."

Oh, she needed him all right. The fingers of one hand slid seductively down her stomach, through the triangle of curls above her clit. She touched herself, stroked her clit, slid her fingers into the wet heat dripping from her core. "Here," she said. "I need you here."

He pressed her legs wider, callused fingers brushing up and down her thighs, slow and seductive. His lashes lowered, head tilted as he watched her caress her sensitive flesh, until he covered her hand with his. Helped her touch herself. "Keep going," he said, urging her to caress her swollen clit, while he slid his finger inside her. Katie gasped, pleasure sparking through her. He slid another finger inside, delicately exploring. His lips trailed along her upper thigh, teasing her with where they might go next. Tongue tracking a line along the triangle.

"Luke!" Katie said, going insane from the anticipation, arching her hips, pressing against his fingers.

"Is this what you want?" he asked, leaning in and kissing her fingers as they slid along her nub. "My mouth?"

"Yes," she gasped. "Yes."

"Say it," he demanded.

"I want your mouth," she said.

"Where?"

"On me," she said, beyond shyness now. "Inside me. All over me."

Her reward was instant. His mouth replaced her hand, covering her clit with warm, wet heat as he gently suckled her. A moment later, he was licking her, tasting her, driving her wild.

Her hands covered her breasts, molding them, caressing them, even as Luke's tongue pierced the intimate folds of her body, mimicking sex, driving her wild. Katie couldn't stay still, her hips pumping against him, hands laced in his hair with a damn near desperate need to hold him there until she found release. Until his fingers, his mouth, pressed her over the edge. She tensed, her body stiff before the eruption. He took her to the very last color in that fascinating rainbow of release, then he laid the two of them down on the couch, side by side, his steely-hard erection slipping between her legs.

"Do you have any idea how much I want to be inside you right now?" he asked.

"Then why aren't you?" she responded, loving the feel of him pressed so close, her back to the couch, her front to him. But even still, in some far corner of her lust-fogged mind, Katie realized the significance of their position, of Luke's care of her comfort and her leg, despite his obvious arousal. It meant something, but right now she didn't know what.

Right now, all she could process was how hard he was, and how close to being inside her. A second later, he was inside her, buried deep to her core. Their eyes locked, her hand sliding to the side of his face. Something emotional joined them, a connection that she felt in her chest, and in the way her body clenched his cock. The way she wanted him deeper—wanted him to move in her. And in that split second, Katie wasn't sure he could ever be deep enough.

LUKE GROGGILY WOKE to the sound of rain and a dull pounding in the distance. He blinked and took in the dimly lit den, smiling as he found Katie snuggled next to him, lying on her stomach, her pearly-white ass displayed for his admiration. The knocking sounded again, a distant muffled cell phone ring humming in the air, as well. Suddenly, Luke snapped to alertness, fully recovering from his satisfied sleep, a product of another amazing lovemaking session on the couch.

"Katie," he said softly, running his hand through

her hair. "Wake up, sweetheart. I think your men are here."

Her head lifted. "What? Oh. Oh!" She jumped into a sitting position, her movements jerky and rushed. "Where are my clothes?" She stood. "The den!" She took off running, naked, gorgeous.

Luke could do nothing more than sit there, stunned, aroused, wanting. He stared down at his cock, fast on the rise. "Down, boy." Then he pushed to his feet and headed after her. His clothes were still in the den, as well.

Luke found Katie already nearly dressed when he arrived. She grabbed his jeans and shoved them at him. "In less than a day, we've been busted without clothes two times. Good grief, how does that happen?" A smile touched Luke's lips as he stepped into his pants. "Are you smiling?" she demanded, slipping on her shoes.

"Of course not," he claimed innocently. "Why would any man smile after having you naked and moaning his name, not once, but many times, in one day?"

She had shoved her hands on her hips and opened her mouth in what was sure to be a reprimand when her cell phone started ringing on the table. Adjusting her clothes, she then pointed. "Put your shirt on. They must be calling because we aren't answering the door. I'm going to let them in!"

She started to dart away, and Luke caught her. She pushed at his chest. "Luke! They're getting rained on!"

He planted a short, firm kiss on her lips. "You might want to turn your shirt around in the right direction."

Katie's jaw dropped and she looked down. "Oh, my

God." She scrambled, trying to get out of the shirt, and it twisted into a mess. "I can't get it right." She pressed her hand to her head. "Luke!"

"Easy, sweetheart," Luke said sweetly and took the shirt, turning it correctly for her.

She snatched it and pulled it over her head, then ran her hands over her hair. "Am I okay? Do I look like... we—"

He arched an eyebrow. "Had mind-blowing sex?"

"Luke!" she muttered.

His lips twitched. "Okay," he said playfully. "No. You don't look like you just had mind-blowing sex. You look like you need to."

She grimaced, but the heat in her gaze said she wasn't angry. "Put your boots on," she ordered, and started to turn away then hesitated. "Luke. My guys are only here until Texas. I don't—"

"Want them to know about the mind-blowing sex," he said. "Check. No problem." But even as he said the words, it felt like a problem.

Katie stopped, as if she understood his reservations. "Luke?"

Luke grabbed his boots and quickly put them in place. "It's fine, Katie," he said. "Go let them in."

She paused another moment and then sped from the room. Katie's team was here to catch his stalker, which meant he had to deal with the fact that he had a stalker. Worse, he had to put on a show and pretend he wouldn't prefer to just get Katie naked again.

LESS THAN AN HOUR LATER, Luke sat at his kitchen table with Katie and her two men, Noah and Josh, and despite it being well after the midnight hour, he listened to plans to evaluate his security, as well as every person he'd ever come in contact with. Katie had a list of questions she'd reviewed with him and a spreadsheet of every player on the team. It was enough to have made Luke damn glad to have the distraction of a pizza delivery.

"I thought you baseball players only ate chicken breast and stuff like that," Josh said, reaching for his fifth piece of pizza. He sported a buzz cut and clean-shaven jaw that said he'd shaved at least twice that day—obviously a habit formed in the SEALs. Noah, his older brother by five years, was an extreme opposite, with long, dark hair tied at his neck and a beard at least two days old.

"Hey," Katie scolded. "You say that like he's an alien from another planet."

"Forgive him," Noah said, giving Josh an irritated look. "Despite being incredibly smart, he can be an absolute *idiot*."

"High-and-mighty asshole," Josh grumbled under his breath about his brother, before flipping open a pizza box.

Luke laughed and exchanged an amused look with Katie. Luke finished off a fourth slice of pizza before slapping another loaded slice onto his plate. He'd forgotten how hungry good sex made him, he'd been in such a dry spell. "I do a five-day, clean-eating cycle. Five on, two off. Keeps me sane."

"Whatever you do, man," Josh said. "It's working, so keep doing it. You rock out there on the field." He snagged a piece of pepperoni from atop his pizza slice and swallowed it. "I'll never forget that showdown between you and Crawford in game three of the playoffs.

That had to be a sweet victory. Crawford talked all kinds of trash about how easy your pitches were to hit and then you shut him down flat." A look of male appreciation filled his face. "How fast was that last pitch you laid on him?"

Luke shrugged, already halfway through his current slice of pizza. "He didn't hit it," he said. "That's all that matters."

"Ninety-five," Noah said. "The pitch was clocked at ninety-five."

Absently, Luke took a sip of iced tea. He'd been in his zone that day. He'd been in his zone all that season. "Which means if Crawford would have gotten a hold of it, I would have been screwed." He set the drink down. "He would have flown it clear to my hometown in Texas. The man cracks a mean bat." And Luke would face him again and soon. His gut twisted a little on that thought, a hint of self-doubt sliding into play. He didn't usually let self-doubt surface—it was dangerous and destructive. So was the big ego that a lot of guys developed to hide from that doubt. There was a happy medium between ego and confidence and that was where Luke normally did well. It was part of his success.

"We'll do our job, Luke, and take care of your security, so you can take care of Crawford," Josh offered. "We'll inspect your setup here and make it nice and tight."

"I should have something from the lab on the letters by early in the week," Noah said. "Maybe we can snag this perp before preseason is over. Give you that peace of mind before you face Crawford again."

Josh chimed in again. "Rest assured, we're a pretty good team ourselves. We'll get the job done."

The twist in Luke's gut tightened, and he forced himself to respond nonchalantly, lifting his glass in a mock toast. "To getting the job done, on and off the field."

He could feel Katie's eyes on him as he clinked glasses with Noah and Josh. Luke placed another slice of pizza on his plate and stood up. He'd shown everyone to their rooms earlier. They knew where to go when they were ready and he wasn't in the mood to play host. It's not as if he'd invited them here. This was all forced on him.

"Unless you boys need tucking in, I'm hitting the sack. It's been a long day." He exchanged a few more words with the two guys, but not with Katie, who sat quietly, watching him, far too observant. She knew something was wrong with him. He sensed it. How the woman read him so easily he didn't know. And he wasn't sure how he felt about it, either.

He took the stairs quickly, found his door and was about to enter when he heard, "Luke!"

Turning, he found Katie hobbling after him with her stiff leg slowing her down. Part of him wanted distance from her right now. Another part wanted to hold her close. What he didn't want was to wait for her to climb those stairs. Standing still seemed to twist the knots in his stomach harder. If not for the damn pizza in his hand, he would have gone after her and carried her the rest of the way to the top.

Finally, though, she was in front of him, shoving that dark brown hair from her eyes. He remembered having it on his cheek, on his chest.

She tilted her head. "What's going on, Luke? Did Noah or Josh say something wrong? I know Crawford might be a sore spot."

"No," he said. "Nothing at all. I don't give a rat's ass about Crawford."

She frowned. "Well," she said. "I know Noah and Josh were talking a lot of trash to each other, but—"

"I know they're good at their jobs," he said. "I can tell."

"Is that what this is about? The job thing again?"

"No," he answered. He inhaled a heavy breath, considered avoiding a direct response, but he'd learned enough about Katie in the short time he'd known her to realize that wouldn't fly. "Look. I'm feeling claustrophobic by the extra security."

"They'll only be here a couple of days. We just need to do everything possible to end this mess before your season starts. They can help me do that."

He motioned to the pizza. "Let me put this down." He inclined his head toward his room and didn't give her time to object.

Luke walked into the room, glancing around, seeing it as she might. The truth was, he was a simple guy, without any time or desire to go furniture shopping. The room matched the guest suite. A sleigh bed, navy-blue comforter, same dressers and nightstands. But there were no flowers, no fuss. Luke set his plate on the nightstand, the drink on a coaster.

Katie followed him inside and shut the door, and he watched as she turned toward the picture that consumed the entire wall to his left. His favorite painting of Nolan

Ryan, throwing a fastball. "The best pitcher that ever lived," he said.

She cut him a sideways glance. "I thought you were."

Luke scoffed, sitting down on the bed, his gaze skimming her slender figure, a memory of holding her, of being inside her washing over him. Unbidden, despite his less than stellar mood, his cock twitched. He forced aside the more primal tendencies Katie drew from him and refocused on the picture.

"You're amazing," she said. "To be that good and that grounded." She crossed to the bed and sat down facing him, scooted far enough back on the mattress to stretch out her leg, as if she were completely comfortable in his room, on his bed. And remarkably, he was, too. "There aren't many people who that can be said about." Katie rolled her eyes. "Lord only knows I've been around my share of arrogance. Success breeds it like rabbits."

"Sometimes fear of failure breeds arrogance," he added, repeating what he'd thought to himself at the table. "Once you allow self-doubt, you allow failure."

Katie studied him, those brown eyes brimming with speculation. "What's on your mind, Luke?"

"You've read my press."

"A lot of it," she agreed. "Yes."

"So you know there's speculation about my game," he said. "About all the crap I went through this past year affecting my pitching."

She gave a slow incline of her head. "I did, but honestly I didn't give it that much thought. Not after you seemed so confident about your 'hot zone,' as you called it." She sat up a bit, seeming intent on getting her point across. "If you're worried about more press speculation concerning this stalker, I promise you I am doing everything in my power to make sure it doesn't leak. I trust Noah and Josh, but they will be gone once you're on the road. We'll keep this all low-key, between you and me."

"It's not that," he said. "I know I swore none of this was getting to me, and I believed it. But tonight, your staff is here, staying in my home, about to take it over. It's not just you anymore, a woman I have a personal interest in. It made me realize this stalker situation has taken over my life. That means it can take over my game."

Katie slid up close to him and climbed on his lap.

"Your knee," he objected.

"Is fine," she said, sliding her arms around his neck. "And so are you. I'll make sure of it."

Luke froze, and the absolute panic forming inside him over his game slid away. He was hot and hard, but his heart was soft, melting like butter. Katie made him feel as if she was talking to the man, not the baseball player. He'd never had a woman reach him on that level.

Luke rolled her on her back and slid on top of her. And with her breathless pleas and wet heat surrounding him, for now, at least, everything was better.

9

NEAR TWO O'CLOCK the next day, Luke walked to the passenger side door of his truck in front of the coach's house to help Katie get out. "I can do it, Luke," she said, the minute he opened the door.

"Too bad," he said, stepping closer.

Stubbornly, she set her jaw and tried to reach the pavement on her own.

"Woman!" Luke reprimanded. Grabbing her before she hurt herself, he pulled her soft curves against his hard body. Oh, yeah. He liked those soft curves and he held her there a moment; the thin, red sundress she wore, though perfectly discreet, offered only a thin barrier. Awareness spiked between them and he lowered his voice to a seductive purr. "Help isn't so bad, now, is it?"

"This isn't help," she accused softly, her hands gently pressing into his shoulders before he reluctantly settled her on her feet. Unable to resist while the door still blocked them from view, he let his hand caress a path over her backside.

She reached behind her and covered his hand. "You just wanted an opportunity to do this."

"No," he said truthfully, smiling as he added, "but it's a damn nice bonus to being a gentleman."

"Hey!" a male voice exclaimed. "Stop hiding out behind that truck door with your new woman and get your ass in here!" Luke laughed as he glanced at the porch to find Rick standing there, a beer in hand, as he added, "The game's about to start."

"What game?" Katie asked, as Luke shut the truck door.

"Horseshoes," Luke said. "It's a preseason tradition. We haven't lost an opening day game in ten years, and every one of those years, Coach hosted a barbecue where horseshoes were played. Baseball players are a suspicious bunch. Whatever works, we repeat it." He took her hand. "Ready to meet the team?"

"Yes," she said. "I'm ready."

Luke guided her forward, their fingers entwined. His first time to have a woman here, a woman he wanted by his side, and it had to be under crappy circumstances. That mockery of a story about how they met would be told over and over, and that facade would remind him that Katie had come to be by his side to catch a stalker—his stalker. And after lying awake talking to her for hours the night before, he knew her gut feeling was the same as his. They both believed the stalker was someone close to him, trying to put him off his game, or maybe end his career. That meant whoever was behind this might well be right here, amongst his friends.

They reached the porch and Katie squeezed his hand. He glanced over at her.

"Don't think about it," she whispered, reading him with such amazing accuracy that Luke grabbed her and kissed her.

"Save some of that luck for the pitcher's mound, will you?" Rick teased.

Luke grimaced. "You sure your name isn't Tom?"

Rick and Katie both gave him a baffled look.

"As in, Peeping Tom," Luke added.

"Oh, that was bad," Katie said. "Really bad."

At the same time, Rick grinned and wiggled his eyebrows. "I've never minded a good show."

Katie rolled her eyes as Rick entered the house and they followed. "I can tell this is going to be a guy joke kind of day."

"You have no idea," Luke said. "The fun has only just begun." He winked, his eyes locking with hers, a secret message there for her and her alone that had nothing to do with the barbecue and everything to do with how much he wanted her. "That's a promise."

"I'll hold you to that," she whispered.

Luke smiled, and then he realized, suddenly, how much he wanted today to be about him and Katie, the real them, not about the lies they'd created to catch a stalker.

Luke turned her to face him. "When we go out there and tell our story," he said, "don't convince yourself it's all a game again. This isn't a game."

"No," she said, pressing her hand to his chest. "But the reason behind our little charade isn't, either, Luke. I want you to be safe."

"I believe you," he said. "And that might be why you're here—"

"It *is* why I'm here, Luke. I'm here to protect you."

"No. Today, you're here because I want you here. Whatever else you might be, Katie…you're the woman I want here by my side, as my date. I'd choose to have you here if all the other reasons didn't exist."

Confusion touched her expression. Luke sensed her start to withdraw as she said, "You can't know that."

"Don't do that," he said. "Don't push me away."

"I'm not."

"You are," he insisted. "And I won't let you." He kissed her. "That's a promise, as sure as me making you dessert later. And you can bet I'm going to be thinking about it all afternoon." He ran his hand down her hair. He had no idea why Katie affected him like she did, but it felt good. And unlike Katie, he wasn't going to let the past slow him down, nor was he going to allow it to ruin what had started to grow between them. "Let's eat so we can get on to that dessert, sooner than later."

She rewarded him with a smile, the wall he'd felt her building sliding back down. "Right. Let's eat."

Hand in hand, they made a discreet path down the hall, cautious not to be seen until they reached the kitchen. When they reached the glass door to the back-yard, it swept open as the coach greeted them, guiding them into the gathering of friends and teammates. But that sexy promise they'd shared still lingered, reinforced with each passing glance they shared.

KATIE LOUNGED in a patio chair in the coach's backyard under a shaded awning. With the party well underway, she sat with several other women, experiencing what she considered to be a little piece of hell. Team parties and picnics, she knew from her days with Joey, were always packed with big-breasted women and big-egoed men. One of those big-breasted women was the coach's blonde bombshell of a wife, ten years his junior, Heather Bradshaw, who was down-to-earth and friendly, and unfortunately, ever attentive to Katie. That meant every time Katie had an "I-want-to-grind-my-teeth-clear-to-dust" moment, she was forced to smile her way past it. She did so by thinking about her and Luke and their nights spent together.

Thankfully the questions about her dancing and tours, how she'd met Luke and how she'd injured her knee were somewhat behind her. She'd even managed to throw in a remark about Luke pressuring her to go to Texas for the away series. Katie smiled as Luke won yet another game of horseshoes and Rick cursed him up and down—good-naturedly, of course. The two were clearly close friends. And Luke winning horseshoes, she hoped, was a tiny reminder he was still in control. This stalker of his was not.

Rick's date for the day, Libby Reynolds, grimaced. "Dating Luke gave me a complex. He is always so darn perfect."

Katie whipped around, her eyebrows dipping. Her professional instincts were all but vibrating. "You dated Luke? But now you're seeing his best friend?"

Libby laughed and waved off the concern. "Luke doesn't care, believe me. I filled in when he needed a date for a few functions here and there. I certainly never made it past his front door, let alone one of these back-yard functions by his side. Nobody has, before you."

So Katie had been told by about everyone who'd met

her today, and then they'd drilled her and Luke about their relationship. She felt as if she should have had a flyer printed to hand out, explaining their history. It would have been easier than repeating it fifty times.

"How long have you been seeing Rick?" Katie asked.

"Three months." She eyed Rick, who had been plastered by Luke's side pretty much all afternoon. The two were always together, a kind of brother bond between them. "He's a real teddy bear. Easy to get close to and real lovable." She snorted. "Unlike Luke."

Katie's eyes narrowed. "What does that mean?"

Heather answered. "Luke likes his privacy."

"There's nothing wrong with that," Katie said, finding a bit of defensiveness rise in her.

"Oh, my husband agrees wholeheartedly," Heather chimed in, sipping one of the daiquiris Katie had passed on to keep a clear head.

Libby tugged at her little white tee and adjusted the bow positioned over her cleavage. "You wouldn't know that from all the headlines he created last year," Libby said, her tone hinting at a bit of disdain that Katie couldn't quite dismiss. This chick had dated Luke, and now she was dating Rick. That could mean she was a groupie who'd take any player she could get, or she was trying to stay close to Luke through Rick.

"Please," Heather said, setting her drink down. "That low-life little bitch he was dating was behind all his press. I was certain Luke would never date again after that woman." Her gaze shifted to Katie as she added, "Now, not only is he dating, but he can't keep his eyes off you, Katie. Do tell us your secret to seducing the best catch on the planet."

Katie quirked a brow. Shouldn't she think her husband, not Luke, was the catch? Interesting. Probably nothing, but interesting anyway. Katie laughed. "Love potion number nine," she joked.

"Hmm," Heather said, and winked. "Does it make him frisky? If so, I might have to borrow some for Coach."

Katie laughed. "You just called your own husband Coach."

Heather's eyes twinkled with mischief. "He likes it. He has a thing for power, if you know what I mean."

Okay, then. Heather might not think her husband was a catch, but they had a good sex life. Or an interesting one, it seemed.

Katie was contemplating a response when suddenly Luke's hands settled on her shoulders. A shiver raced down her spine. She looked up at him and found warmth spreading through her body reflected in his tender eyes. "Hey," she said softly, head spinning with the impact of her response to such a small gesture.

He squatted next to her, sliding his hand to her knee. "Hey, yourself. How's it going?" His voice was low, intimate, for her ears only.

"Good," she replied, because nothing else seemed to form on her lips. They stared at each other, millions of emotions welling inside her. She hadn't bargained for this connection with Luke, nor the fact that no amount of logic was allowing her to dismiss it.

"Uh-oh," Heather said. "Carl and Rick are going at each other again."

"Carl Malone," Luke clarified to Katie. "Rookie pitcher brought up from the farm team. Total pain in the ass."

"It would help if you and Rick would stop calling him 'Thumbs,'" Heather chided.

Katie's jaw dropped. "No, you don't. Luke. That's horrible."

"If you knew the trash he talked, you wouldn't say that," Luke assured her. "Everything is someone else's fault. He ignores Conn's calls." Conn being Mike Connelly, the short, stocky catcher from Long Island whom Katie had noticed talked a lot of New York-style trash that generally amused his teammates.

He glanced at Heather. "He ignores Coach. Talks shit behind his back even. We wanted to give the kid a good knock off his high horse in preseason, but it's only a couple of days until their first game on Thursday night, not much of a chance that'll happen."

Luke and Heather continued to debate the best handling of "Thumbs," while Katie scraped the recesses of her brain, trying to recall Malone with more detail. Malone. Yes. Okay. He'd played ball at the University of Texas, like Luke, but years later, of course.

She would have thought that would have built a common bond. Then again, Luke was, no doubt, legendary at UT. The ones who left and became stars always were. Maybe Malone felt he was walking in Luke's shadow then and now. Maybe Malone wanted Luke off the team, so he was trying to screw with Luke's game.

"Yes," Luke said quietly, kneeling before her again. "I've considered what you are thinking."

She focused on Luke and nodded. They had a solid suspect in Malone. That felt like a positive thing.

"Speaking of Malone," Rick said, as he and Conn joined them under the shade. "Thumbs is talking so much crap," Rick said, sitting down next to Libby, "his tongue is going to swell right along with his head."

Heather slapped her hands on her lap. "See what I mean?" she exclaimed, casting Katie a helpless look. "They call him that name, and he gets more fired up."

Conn popped open a beer and motioned to Luke. "He says you're cheating."

Luke laughed, ignoring Heather, as did Conn and Rick. "How do you cheat at horseshoes?"

"Same way every call I make caused him to throw balls, I guess," Conn said. "And he wonders why I say UT hasn't picked a good pitcher since Luke."

Katie cringed. No wonder Luke and Malone didn't share a school bond.

Libby straightened and added, "It wouldn't hurt you to be a bit more humble, Luke."

"It's backyard horseshoes and beer, Libby," Luke said drily. "Egging each other on is part of the fun."

Rick laughed. "Here, here," he agreed, raising his beer in a toast.

"I'm not talking about horseshoes in the backyard," Libby said. "I'm talking in general."

Conn gaped. "Luke's the most humble guy I know."

Rick made a growling sound near Libby's ear. "Down, girl. No biting in the backyard. Save that for the bedroom."

Heather almost choked on her drink. "Rick!"

Katie gaped.

Coach Bradshaw, a tall man with gray hair, broad shoulders and tough, chiseled features, strolled up to join them. "Going for four, Luke?" he asked, referring to the three horseshoe games Luke had already won that day.

Luke pushed to his feet, but his hand remained possessively on Katie's shoulder. "I never speculate, Coach, you know that."

Libby snorted, as if something about Luke's words disgusted her.

"Knock it off, Libby," Rick reprimanded sharply.

"He's getting old," came a male voice. "But then that's why they pulled me in to close up the games all nice and tidy for him."

Katie looked up to find Malone standing there—tall, dark, younger than Rick, and ten pounds lighter. Something about the man scraped down her nerve endings and set her on edge.

"You better close and close well," Luke said, pushing to his feet and snatching a beer from a cooler. "That's why they call this a team. We win together." He tipped his can back. "Stop throwing blame and start throwing some heat. That's the point we've been singing at ya, man, but you keep tuning us out."

"Luke's right, kid," Coach said. "I have a rotation to fill, and I expect every one of you to be the best."

"Coach," yelled one of the players from the sliding glass door. "That PR lady is here to see you."

"Today is not the day to deal with her." He grumbled to his wife, shaking his head. "Why did management have to hire this woman?"

Heather squeezed his hand, and they exchanged a look. "They're heading off problems," she said in a voice that indicated this wasn't her first time to say the words.

"About me," Luke claimed. "Go ahead. Say it. We all know it."

"Yeah," Malone said. "Be nice to make the news about playing ball. Not about Luke's vastly dysfunctional social life."

"Shut up, Malone," Rick spouted.

"Yeah," Coach said roughly. "Shut up, kid." He glanced at Luke. "Don't let any of this get to you, Luke. You're not the only reason management hired PR support. There's plenty of players mustering up bad press. And most of them create it themselves. You couldn't help yours." He glanced at Malone. "Those of us who were actually here know that."

Malone snorted. "Since when is choosing the wrong bedmate not his fault?"

Katie didn't consider that remark might be aimed at her. She wrapped her hand around Luke's arm, silently offering support. Now she knew what Luke meant when he said arrogance was something people hid behind. Unfortunately, she had a feeling there was a whole lot of nasty insecurity underneath Malone's arrogance, the kind that festered and became poison.

"Coach?" the player at the door questioned. "What do I do?"

Coach grunted and waved toward the door. "Keep that woman inside," he yelled. "I'll be right in." He lowered his voice, scrubbing his jaw as he spoke to his wife. "She distracts the players and not much else." His gaze lifted and caught. "Oh, hell, too late. Here she comes."

Katie looked up to find Olivia crossing the lawn, her skirt almost as high as her four-inch spike heels, enough thigh showing to be R-rated. Male eyes latched on to her, a murmuring of male comments rumbling through the air. But Olivia directed her attention one place and one place only. *At Luke.* Who, unlike the other guys, was not drooling. In fact, as before, he didn't seem at all pleased to see Olivia. Olivia, however, Katie realized, appeared quite happy to see Luke, her eyes lighting on him, her lips lifting in a flirty smile.

Jealousy flared in Katie, her stomach tensing. Reprimanding herself, Katie quickly squashed the feeling as ridiculous. She had no claim on Luke's affections. None. It didn't matter how much her feelings for him were growing. In fact, if he wanted Olivia, or anyone else for that matter, so be it. She was more than fine with that.

Self-satisfaction filled Katie, and she reveled in the knowledge that the self-doubt and feelings of inadequacy that her knee injury had created were behind her. Not Luke, or Olivia, or even the dull throb of her knee acting up could make her lose her way again.

Rick and Libby exchanged low, heated words, snapping Katie out of her reverie.

"Enough, Libby," Rick ordered tersely.

Suddenly, Libby was on her feet, and then she did the unthinkable—she burst into tears in front of everyone. "It's not enough," she yelled at him. "That's the point. *I* am never enough for you." She started running toward the house.

Katie's mouth dropped. Libby was clearly not a stable person.

"Oh, hell," Rick muttered under his breath, and eyed Heather for help.

Heather held up her hands. "Don't look at me. I'm not going after her. This gets older and older every time."

Luke shook his head. "Man, why do you mess with her?"

Rick ran a rough hand over his head. "What can I say?" he said. "She's like crack. A bad high I can't seem to get enough of."

"That's going to make you self-destruct," Luke warned.

Katie sighed. "I'll go after her."

Luke looked surprised. "You sure about that?" he asked.

She lowered her voice purposely. "I think it would be good for me to get to know her." They exchanged a look of understanding. Libby was climbing her way up the Luke-obsessed suspect list. Katie needed to understand what was going on in that woman's head.

Luke reluctantly nodded. "Watch your back with her."

"Always," Katie assured him, just as Olivia tore herself away from the coach and stopped in front of them, casting Katie a disapproving look and then focusing on Rick.

"Looks like we have some potential bad press to discuss about your present dating habits," Olivia commented sarcastically. She glanced at Libby's departing form, disapproval etched in her perfectly painted features. "What happens when she does this kind of thing in front of a reporter?"

"On second thought," Luke murmured to Katie. "Maybe I should go with you to check on Libby."

She shook her head and laughed. "You're staying," she ordered and squeezed his hand. "Let the power of the force be with you, Yoda."

THE BATHROOM SEEMED the logical place for a crying female to go. Katie had dealt with her sister enough to know the drill. Though not at first glance, it was now clear Libby had some of Carrie's traits; namely, and most obviously, a selfish need for attention.

As she made her way through the country-style, multistoried house, Katie wished she had asked where the closest bathroom could be found. There were rooms upstairs, rooms downstairs, rooms on the main level. She was left guessing which way would be the right way, and she decided up seemed likely.

Upstairs was dark but that didn't deter Katie. The compact purse she had strapped across her chest had a cell phone and a small handgun. Not that she would readily consider whipping out a weapon, here or anywhere for that matter, but it was comforting to know it was resting by her side, ready for use.

As her eyes adjusted, she began checking several doorways, including that of a spare bathroom, finding no sign of Libby. She was about to switch directions when a shattering sound echoed through the silence, seeming to come from the door at the end of the hallway. Following the noise, her hand instinctively on her purse, Katie pursued the sound down the corridor and entered a massive bedroom, with fancy antique-looking furniture and expensive paintings. A quick scan indicated she was alone, so Katie proceeded toward the entrance to the bathroom.

Peering cautiously through the doorway, she found flower buds among broken glass in the middle of the black-tiled floor. Glass chunks had splattered around the room in a wide enough range to indicate the vase had hit the ground hard, clearly thrown. At least, that was Katie's best guess. Seemed a good indicator that Libby had been here, considering her volatile departure from the backyard.

Whoever was responsible had exited the door on the opposite side of the room, through a second door that appeared to join a smaller room lined with bookcases. Katie had walked toward the vase, intending to pick it up so no one would get hurt, when the door slammed behind her. She jumped and whirled toward the door. Reaching for the knob and pulling, she found it was locked. Her eyes went to the lock. It was on the inside. That meant someone had jammed the door from the outside.

She leaned against the door trying to think, keeping the opposite entrance in sight. She considered calling Luke's cell, but she didn't want him to freak out and somehow alert people of a problem that could snowball into telling them all about his stalker.

This had to be Libby. The woman didn't have much concept of public appropriateness, and she was possibly still hung up on Luke. It meant she probably felt threatened by Katie. The idea of Libby writing those letters was easy to conceive.

A loud thump hit the door directly behind her, making her jump and whirl to face the sound. Immediately she looked over her shoulder at the other door, and called, "Who's there? Libby? Libby, I wanted to talk to you. That's all."

A long silence.

She leaned against the wall, trying to keep both entrances in sight, looking from one to the other, nerves jumping around in her stomach.

Libby, or someone else, was outside one of the doors—but which one?

The silence ended with a hushed whisper that wasn't clearly male or female. "Go away, bitch. We don't like you here."

Goose bumps surfaced on her skin. There was something about the presence…a real darkness that didn't quite fit Libby. Whoever this was didn't play games.

Willing herself to get a grip, she took a deep, calming breath. Okay, that was it. She unzipped her purse and had snagged her cell phone when Luke's voice lifted in the air. "Katie?"

In a flash of movement, she was pounding on the wooden surface, calling his name. "Luke! In here! I'm in here!"

"What in the hell?" she heard him mutter, feeling relief just hearing his voice again, knowing he had heard her. "Katie?"

"Yeah," she called through the door, trying to sound calm. "Get me the hell out of here, will you?"

Moments later the door opened, and Katie launched herself at the opening. Luke caught her arms, facing her. "What's going on?"

She looked over his shoulder. "Did you see anyone when you came down the hall?"

Concern etched his features. "No one," he said. "When Libby returned and you didn't, I came looking for you. Someone stuck a hanger in the lock of the door. What happened?"

"Was anyone else missing from the backyard?"

He shook his head. "I don't know. I don't think so."

She pressed her hand to her head, trying to think of anything of use. "I don't know what happened exactly. Someone locked me inside. They told me to get away and stay away. The question is—do they want me gone because I'm supposed to be dating you or because they know who I really am? And before you ask, no, I didn't recognize the voice. It was muffled."

"Male or female?"

She shook her head. "I don't know."

He pulled her close and kissed her. When he stopped, he looked into her eyes. "Katie. I never meant to put you in danger." He seemed shaken. "What if I am putting other people in danger? What if… Maybe I shouldn't be traveling with the team."

She pressed her hand to his face. "It might come to that," she said reluctantly, "but we're not there yet. You pitch that great season you're after. Let me and my team make this go away. If we can't or if things get worse, then and only then will we talk about you taking some time off. Now, let's go back down to the party where we belong."

He drew her hand from his cheek to his lips. "I say we get the hell out of here," he said. "Go find our own afternoon diversion."

As tempting as his offer sounded, Katie had to consider the psychological profile of this person with her team. The safest thing in her mind was to go on with the rest of the party as if all was normal. She didn't want to send this person running for the hills where they couldn't catch him or her. Nor did she want to set off anger that turned to violence.

She pressed her lips to his. Then, "We aren't being run off from the party any more than you are the mound. Not if I have any say-so in the matter."

His eyes lit and turned dark, his voice raspy, affected. His hand slid over her lower back, molding her close. "Have I told you I'm crazy about you?"

She smiled. "Mostly you've told me I make you crazy."

"That, too," he said. "But I like crazy. I like crazy one hell of a lot."

So did she. And though she knew there were all kinds of reasons she shouldn't, she couldn't think of one of them right here and now.

When finally they headed back to the party, Katie reported the broken vase to Heather, who charged toward the house to inspect the damage. Katie sat down in a lawn chair as Luke went back to his horseshoes, and she inventoried what she'd learned. Jessica wasn't at the party, which all but eliminated her from the suspect list, assuming the bathroom encounter had been with the stalker. Olivia had been in the backyard talking with Rick so that pretty much ruled out both of them. Ron wasn't even present to be considered as a suspect, not that she'd ever really considered him. He was a heavy-handed manager and a manipulator, but she doubted he was behind the letters. As for the agent trying to connect with Luke at the charity benefit—turned out to have an excuse to be there besides stalking Luke. Sadly, he had a sister with leukemia. Libby, on the other hand, was concerning in all kinds of ways. And she'd disappeared without saying goodbye to anyone. She was volatile, illogical.

Libby had become her prime suspect—at least for locking her in the bathroom. There was always the chance that there was no connection between what had happened in that bathroom and the letters. An unlikely chance, but still a chance. Katie glanced at Luke and realized she was no closer to figuring out who was threatening him, but there was one thing she *was* closer to—and that was falling for Luke. He was the one making *her* crazy.

IT WAS close to ten that same night, and Katie had been at the kitchen table with Josh and Noah, reviewing Luke's file and talking through security plans for several hours, when Luke quietly snuck into the kitchen and snatched a bottle of water. He wore sweats and a snug T-shirt, and had sexy, masculine stubble brushing his jaw.

His gaze slid to Katie's as if he sensed she was watching him. Instant awareness crackled between them, his eyes lingering on hers before he silently slipped out of the room.

Katie quickly cut her gaze back to the file, delicately clearing her throat. "Okay, so tomorrow the new security system arrives and—"

"At least your cover's going to be believable," Noah said quietly.

Katie looked up to find them both staring at her. "What?"

"You and Luke. We aren't stupid, Katie. We can see you two have something going on."

Her first reaction was denial, but Katie squashed it. Noah and Josh were too smart for that. "It's unprofessional," she said. "I know, and—"

"You're afraid it's a distraction," he said.

She nodded. "Yes."

"Fighting anything as obvious as what you two have, while you try and *play* boyfriend and girlfriend," Noah said. "That's a distraction. Use it, Katie. Make it work for you. Use the insight to Luke to find this person who's turning his life upside down." He pushed to his feet, leaving her to the files and her own thoughts.

Josh stood, as well, and then grinned. "Do your part to keep that man focused on something other than the letters so he can get on that mound and fire away."

Noah grabbed Josh's arm and tugged him along, grumbling a remark in the process.

Katie sat there, her emotions twisting and turning, before she took the file and headed to the den where Luke had been watching replays of preseason baseball games for hours.

She found him on the leather sofa—the sofa they'd made love on—his back to the door. Memories washed over her, of them together, of the passion. And she knew she wasn't going to deny she wanted Luke. Wasn't going to let herself run or hide as he'd once accused her.

He turned around. "Hey," he said, and quickly switched off the television. "Everything okay?"

"Yes," she said softly. "I need…" Him. But she didn't

say that. Not yet. Business first. She sauntered toward him, aware of his hot stare following her. She joined him on the sofa, a few inches separating them.

"You need...?" he prodded gently, more of the crackling sexual tension from the kitchen flaring between them.

"I need you to tell me about your years in the pros. Maybe it will trigger some bit of information I can use for the investigation."

He nodded slowly. "I'll tell you anything you want to know, Katie," he said. "As long as you promise to tell me anything I want to know."

Her chest tightened at the ultimatum. Anything was right up there with everything, and she wasn't sure she still had that to give to anyone, not even Luke.

When she didn't immediately respond, he leaned forward, still not touching her though his lips lingered by her ear, his breath warm. "Why did you really come in here?" he whispered. "What is it you really need?"

Her pulse sped up as she whispered, "You."

"Do you now?" he challenged.

"Yes," she said, reaching for him. He shackled her hands.

"Oh, no," he murmured. "You touch when I tell you to touch. Get undressed while I lock the door."

Shaking with that need she'd confessed, Katie did as Luke ordered, amazingly aroused by the added intimacy and vulnerability of her confession.

He returned and scooted the coffee table out of the way before sitting down. "Come here," he told her, his gaze raking over her naked body with such intimacy she could feel the dampness gathering between her thighs, the heat pooling low in her stomach. He pulled her between his thighs and kissed her stomach. She reached for his hair, and he set her hands away. "No touching."

"Luke," she whimpered.

"Here's how this is going to work," he said. "I'm going to show you just how much you need me. To be sure you never forget."

And he proceeded to do so, oh, so well. Katie sighed as his mouth closed over her clit, suckling and licking and taking her to the edge for the first of many times that night. She had no idea where this was going with Luke, but hours later, after he'd driven her to the edge, punished her with blissful pleasure, she wasn't willing to deny it still wasn't enough. She needed more.

10

THE STALKER WAS silent for three days after Katie and Luke came out of the proverbial relationship closet, ten days total. Luke's house was well secured, the top suspects were being investigated and monitored, and everything was otherwise calm. A good thing, since Luke was pitching the first at-home, season game that night. The best case, the stalker had lost interest in Luke. The worst case, well, Katie didn't want to think about the many possibilities.

It was early morning yet, and since Katie still couldn't run, Luke and Katie had started the day with a swim as they had the two days before. They'd then tossed shorts over their suits to begin making breakfast, another little ritual they'd formed. As if they were a couple. And maybe they were.

Katie had mixed feelings. She wanted this case over; she wanted Luke safe. But what happened when he was traveling and she went home? Was their relationship simply a bridge through troubled times for each other or were they more than that? A temporary need that fulfilled something they both craved on some personal level?

Rick, Noah and Josh were all gathered at the table, chowing down on eggs, sausage and pancakes. They apparently felt this was their ritual, as well, taking advantage of Luke's willingness to cook.

Katie looked forward to watching him pitch, never mind cooking, though there was no denying there was a subtle tension mingled with hope in the house as everyone speculated about the stalker's silence.

Grabbing the coffeepot, Luke filled a couple of mugs meant for himself and Katie. Josh managed to cross the kitchen with lightning speed and claim one of them.

"Thanks, man," he said. "I needed this." He sauntered back to the table and cast Rick a look. "Me and Noah were up all night monitoring Rick's psycho girlfriend, among others."

Rick grimaced and took the coffee cup from Josh. "Libby is not my girlfriend," he said. "I broke up with her."

Noah let out a bark of laughter. "Until he decides he needs another easy booty call."

Josh snorted. "Yeah."

Luke and Katie exchanged an amused look. "Hey!" Katie exclaimed indignantly, to no avail. Both she and Luke had lost their mugs.

Noah acted unaffected, sipped from the mug and continued to talk. "At least Libby doesn't seem to be writing the letters or even secretly mutilating animals. So far she's stuck with terrorizing barbecues and—after following her yesterday, from what I can tell—shoe stores.

She spent three hours in one yesterday. I was in hell and so were the salespeople."

Katie held up her hands in protest. "Please. Keep the booty-call talk to yourself. And you know how I feel about Libby. Keep watching her. She's our person. I feel it in my gut."

"All I feel in my gut," Josh said, forking a pancake, "is the need for more food." He dropped the pancake onto his plate. "That and I have a bad feeling about Jessica that no one else seems to get."

Noah finished his coffee. "She's too young and too naive to be conniving enough to pull off all these letters and not make a mistake that gets her caught."

Katie chimed in her agreement with Noah. "I'm sticking with Libby." She eyed Rick. "Good thing you're not."

"Man, Katie," Rick said. "Ever since I made you mad at the benefit, you've been on my ass."

Katie studied him seriously as she accepted a cup of coffee from Luke. "And that covers the entire time I've known you. You ballplayers are all about superstitions. If I start being nice now, it might be unlucky. I better keep busting your chops every chance I get."

LUKE CHUCKLED at the exchange. Having Katie here felt…well, right. Like she belonged. Like she'd been here a lot longer than she had. He set his cup on the counter and pulled her close. "Speaking of superstitions," he said. "You do realize if I pitch well tonight, the game-day breakfast becomes a lucky tradition, to be repeated?"

Katie rolled her eyes. "I swear you ballplayers are all a little obsessive-compulsive."

"Let them be OCD or whatever they need to be to win," Josh said. The doorbell rang. Josh pushed his chair back and looked disgusted. "Ah, no. Someone else heard about breakfast and thinks they are getting pancakes. Forget it. There aren't enough to go around."

Noah pushed to his feet, cup in hand. "I'll get the door. I need a refill anyway."

Luke rubbed his hands together as he finished the last of the cooking. "Finally," he said. "I think we're ready to sit down and eat."

"I couldn't agree more," Katie said. "I'm starving."

Noah reappeared with Ron by his side. "You might want to wait on that food."

"Another letter," Ron said, holding up a plastic, sealed bag.

"I'll get it to the lab," Noah offered. "And hope for more than the generalizations they gave me last week. Maybe we'll get a fingerprint this time."

Luke leaned against the counter, the air knocked right out of him. He glanced around the kitchen. "So much for a good-luck tradition. You know what? You guys do your thing. Eat. Investigate. Whatever. I can't think about this on game day." Which would be easier without a couple of tech guys sharing breakfast with him, reminding him he was under lock and key. "I'm going to take a shower." No one objected or tried to stop him, and he was damn glad.

He disappeared into his room, shut the door and headed to the shower. Stripping off his swim trunks and T-shirt, he stepped under the hot water. Damn it. "Why today?" he whispered.

"Because today is game day." It was Katie's voice, soft and close, right outside the curtain. It moved and suddenly she was inside, naked, beautiful, the distraction he needed. "Don't you see?" she asked, stepping right up to him and twining her arms around him. "Whoever sent that letter knew you were pitching today. They knew it couldn't be ignored. Not if your safety was going to be considered. This person wanted to be sure you got it today. They wanted to rattle you. So don't give them that satisfaction. Go pitch your best game ever." She kissed his chest, then kissed his lips. "And I was thinking of a new game-day tradition."

She was soft and perfect in his arms, and he was hard and hot for her. He was crazy about her. Hell. He was pretty sure he was in love with her. "What new tradition?"

She smiled, her palm caressing his chest as she slowly slid down his body and went to her knees. His breath hitched as her hand closed around his erection. His muscles corded, tensed, as her tongue flickered around the head of his cock, her gentle fingers caressing his balls and closing around them. Suddenly, there were no letters, there was no pressure to deal with, aside from that pulsing through his balls.

She drew him into her mouth, suckled the sensitive head of his erection, her tongue swirling, licking, teasing. "Katie," he whispered, his hand trying to guide her to take all of him.

But the witch took her time, took him slowly. Her hand tightened around the width of him at the base of his cock, and she slid her lips down him until her mouth met her fingers. And then she stopped moving, lavished him with her tongue. And then she began a tantalizing rhythm, a slow slide backward, a slow slide forward, until his hips were thrusting against her. Pleasure ripping through him, release building inside him. Building. Building. Explosive. A tight sensation traveled down his spine and settled at the base of his cock. On edge, close to release, he struggled with self-restraint. "Katie," he gasped, "stop. Before I can't stop."

She suckled him deeper, pumped him with her hand. He cried out, tried to stop her, tried, but felt the wildness in him. The need. Warm water sprayed around his back, white-hot desire through his limbs. She sucked him deeper, used her lips, her tongue, her hand. Luke was beyond thinking, beyond control. Katie had all of him. His release thundered from inside him, an explosion so fierce it shook him, so complete he lost all sense of self. There was only the pleasure. And the gentle swirls of her tongue as she drew him to completion.

When finally she slid up his body and pressed those soft curves to him, Luke decided there was no pregame tradition better than one that included Katie naked in his arms. Nor any better way to spend the day than making love to her. And that was exactly what he intended to do.

KATIE SAT in the stands with Josh, Noah and Heather surrounding her as the first game of the season neared the end, most certainly a victory for the Hawks after Luke pitched five no-run innings.

"I can't believe I thought baseball was boring," Katie

said, talking to Heather, who sat to her right. "Watching Luke square off with those batters had my heart beating a mile a minute."

"There certainly wasn't a more perfect game for your brothers to attend," Heather said, smiling as she glanced to Katie's left where Noah and Josh sat. "I'd say the coaching and pitching have been exceptional."

Katie smiled, having decided Heather was very much in love with her husband. "Indeed," Katie agreed. "And they're here the rest of the week, so they'll get to see him pitch once more in the rotation."

"Oh, how wonderful," Heather said. "And you're even learning the game now. I'm impressed. We'll turn you into an expert before you know it." She winked. "We'll have them thinking you're a regular groupie in no time."

Katie choked on that one. "Oh, please, no."

Heather laughed. She explained how she hated the groupie scene; her husband liked them even less, as he felt the women were a negative distraction to his team.

Josh patted his stomach and leaned toward Katie. "Nachos didn't do the job. Going to grab a candy bar before the concession stand closes." Code for *going to get a broader view of the stadium as the game draws to conclusion*. Bringing them along had been a precaution after the letter. They were all frustrated that they'd made no progress so far besides securing the house and analyzing certain people of interest.

A few minutes later, Katie stood outside the locker room with Noah by her side, Josh still MIA. "Someone is driving to different post office locations and mailing these letters," Katie said, her voice low. "We need to catch them in the act. Prove they were at the exact post office as one of the letters received. It has to be Jessica, Libby or Malone. We need them under surveillance."

"We can GPS their cars," Josh suggested. "It's the simplest solution. I'd also suggest we hang back here when you head to Texas. We'll stay at a hotel and covertly monitor Luke's house and our suspect list. Whoever is behind this might make careless mistakes when they think no one is around to watch."

"Agreed," Katie said, her cell ringing from inside her purse. She'd have to talk to Ron, but he'd agree, she was certain.

Katie reached for her bag and dug out her cell. "And call that FBI pal of yours and find out what is taking so long on that analysis." She quickly eyed the phone's screen, noting the "unknown" caller ID, and then eyed Noah.

"Another call?" he asked.

Almost daily, she'd been receiving the heavy breathing calls, a poisonous reminder that all was not well at home, either, despite Donna's assurances that she had things under control and was watching over Katie's sister and the office.

Katie nodded confirmation, her stomach knotted. "Could the timing stink any worse?"

Noah held out his hand. "Give me the phone," he demanded.

"No," she refused. "I don't want to risk making this worse by refusing their calls. You know that's why I haven't changed my number."

Suddenly, Malone was out of the locker room and

the press swarmed him. Katie hesitated and shoved her phone back into her purse. The questions were coming hard and fast. *"What did you think about tonight's game?"*

"When will we see you pitch?"

"How's it feel to be mentored by Luke Winter?"

"Mentoring me?" Malone asked. "I'm mentoring him."

Laughter erupted, the reporters assuming Malone was joking. He wasn't.

The doors to the locker room opened.

"Luke! Luke!" The reporters were going nuts, and they all turned toward him to pepper him with questions.

It took a good five tension-filled minutes for Luke to peel himself away from the reporters and appear by Katie's side, freshly showered and grinning like a kid in a candy store.

Katie felt the tension inside her slide away at his happiness. He'd been so nervous about today, though he'd admitted it to no one but her.

"You found that zone of yours," she said. "Congratulations."

He pulled her close and kissed her, then spoke softly. "I've decided making love to you before I pitch is lucky. Actually, I think making love to you before and after is lucky. Let's get out of here." He drew her hand in his and tugged her toward the truck.

Katie's mind and body screamed "yes" to the idea of finding her way into Luke's strong arms, him buried inside her, leaving no room for anything but pleasure.

Deep down, she knew she needed tonight, too.

Everything was on the verge of spinning out of control, and she had a horrible knot in her stomach, warning her that a crash was on its way.

11

THE TEXAS SERIES WAS behind them without any incidents. The Hawks' record to date: four wins out of six games. Noah and Josh were convinced the letter writer was someone from the team who couldn't mail a letter from Texas without being obvious. They'd test that theory soon enough with a three-day home series starting again after two days off.

"Watch how he cuts under the fastball," Luke's father, J.C., said to the television, his voice penetrating the kitchen door where Katie sat with Luke's mother, Ann. J.C. continued, "See! Every time! You throw him some heat, boy."

"They can spend hours critiquing the players," Ann warned, her green eyes twinkling, her silvery-gray hair brushing her shoulders. "My husband retired from coaching three years ago, here in Austin, when I left teaching. Sometimes, I think he didn't get the memo. I hope you're not in a rush to leave." The timer on the oven went off.

"You're making chocolate macaroons," Katie said. "I'm not going anywhere." She liked Ann and J.C., and she could see why Luke had insisted on keeping the stalker a secret. They were so happily retired. And so very proud as parents. "My mother used to make macaroons."

Ann pulled the tray from the oven and set it out to cool. "Used to?" Ann asked.

"I lost my parents in a car accident a few years ago," Katie explained, pushing to her feet. "Let me help you with the chocolate."

"Oh, dear," Ann exclaimed, shoving the oven closed. "Honey, I'm sorry. I would never have made these if I'd known your mother made them."

"Oh, Ann," she said. "My mother made macaroons to make me smile. She'd expect nothing less today."

A warm look crossed Ann's face before she inclined her head. "Then let's get that chocolate on top so we can get to eating."

It was a good two hours later when Katie sat on Luke's old bed in the middle of his old bedroom where Spiderman and Troy Aikman decorated the walls; Ann sat across from her.

She and Ann had talked for hours. It turned out Ann had been a grief counselor for teens, and somehow, Katie had started talking about her sister and then never stopped. It was the first time she'd talked—really talked—about losing her parents since their deaths.

"Please tell me she didn't pull out the photo albums," Luke said, appearing in the doorway.

Katie looked up, her stomach fluttering at the country-boy sex appeal he oozed in faded jeans and a light blue button-down Western shirt that highlighted his eyes.

"I most certainly did not," Ann assured him. "I

promised her I would next time, though." She patted Katie's jean-clad leg. "Incentive for you to come back."

Katie smiled at Ann, but she couldn't bring herself to look at Luke. She had no idea how he felt about the invitation. As much as she'd enjoyed the day, her heart was heavy with memories, her emotions twisted.

It wasn't long until Katie was given a bear hug by J.C., who, wearing his Hawks jersey with his son's number on it, was a good six-four and as broad as he was tall. "You come back here, little girl. Nice to see my son finally bring someone home."

Katie smiled. "I'd like that." After the visit, there was no question about why Luke had wanted to keep his parents in the dark about his stalker. They'd be worried sick if they knew. But they also had no idea Katie was here because Luke had no option but to bring her along.

Would Luke have invited her if circumstances were different? She wasn't sure he could answer that at this point. How did either of them know what was real and what was close proximity and circumstances?

As they exited the house, Katie was still avoiding eye contact with Luke. Emotions she hadn't felt in years were stirring to life. Caring for someone and fearing she'd lose them had kept her single for years now.

Luke laced his fingers with hers as they walked to the car in silence. At the passenger side of the car, he slid his hands down her arms, facing her. "You okay, sweetheart? Did my parents say something to upset you?"

"No," she said, shaking her head. "Your parents are wonderful. I love them."

"Then what is it? What's wrong?"

"I…" She felt the emotion flutter in her chest. "I… Luke."

His fingers laced in one side of her hair. "What? Talk to me, Katie."

She blinked up at him, the streetlight illuminating the concern in his eyes. She kissed him. "Memories," she said. "That's all. The family setting stirred some old memories. But it was good talking to your mother."

"You can talk to me, too," he said, his thumbs gently caressing her cheek. "You know that, right?"

"I know," she said. And she did. "But I…can't."

"Why?" he asked. "Am I a bad listener? You don't trust me?"

"No," she said quickly. "No. I…don't want to lay all this heavy stuff on you, Luke. You have games, and—"

He kissed her, a long, deep kiss that left her gasping for air and pressing against his chest. "Luke! Your parents!"

"Are probably cheering from the window," he said. "They loved you. Now. Let's go back to the hotel. I have ways to make you talk."

And just like that, amazingly, Katie was smiling, her demons slayed by a pitcher who had a ninety-eight-mile-an-hour fastball and was one hell of a kisser.

THE FIRST GAME NIGHT back in California, Katie felt edgy, certain something was going to happen. A knack for gut feelings that she'd inherited from her father was something she never ignored. Although she'd kept her worries from Luke. He was pitching the first game, and he needed to be focused. For safety measures, Josh and Noah were in a nearby van, with a remote feed on several locations.

Katie once again sat with Heather and, despite her nerves, cheered excitedly as Luke pitched. "He's going to have his best game ever if he keeps this up," Heather declared. She glanced behind her. "Good grief. I didn't know Libby was here. I do believe Rick really has a thing for that girl. At least when he's in town."

"Come to think of it," Katie said. "I didn't see him with anyone else in Texas. Yet I'm not sure I would have known otherwise. Luke and I didn't exactly hang out with the guys."

Heather elbowed Katie and smiled. "I bet you didn't."

Katie smiled but a grim thought occurred. It would be horrible if Libby ended up being the stalker if Rick was really hung up on her.

The crowd went nuts as the Hawks headed onto the field again and Luke strode toward the mound. Nerves fluttered in Katie's stomach. Her cell phone rang.

She reached inside her purse and eyed the caller ID, almost relieved to see "unknown." They were almost paid up with the loan sharks, and Katie could finally end that piece of hell. She hit Silent as Luke threw a strike.

"Yes!" she yelled, when her phone started to ring again.

A weird flutter, that gut feeling she got sometimes, hit her stomach. She snatched the phone again. Noah. She snapped it open.

"Come out to the parking lot," she thought he said,

as the crowd roared. Luke threw another strike. Katie wasn't cheering. She didn't get a chance to confirm Noah's request. He'd hung up.

"I'll be right back, Heather."

"But Luke is pitching," she argued.

"I know," she said. "I'll be right back."

Heather frowned but Katie didn't offer more. She rushed up the stairs and through the stadium, dialing Noah as she did. When he didn't answer, she started to panic. She rushed out to the parking lot, to where the dark blue van Noah had rented was parked, and headed to the back door.

It opened as she arrived to reveal Noah, squatting down to her eye level. Josh sat at a monitor, his attention on the security feed.

"What?" she demanded.

"First," Noah said. "Your sister and Donna are fine."

Her heart thundered in her ears. "What does that mean?"

"The office was set on fire," he said. "We lost everything. The loan sharks said it's a warning. They want the rest of their money now."

Her office. Destroyed. The only thing she had left. Her dancing was gone. Her parents were gone. "We were paying!" she yelled.

"I know, Katie," he said. "I know. But these kinds of people aren't reasonable. You have insurance. We'll find a temporary office. I'll go home while Josh wraps up here. But, Katie. We need to pay these guys off. You need to talk to Luke. Borrow the money."

"No," she said instantly. "I'm not talking to Luke, and you aren't, either, nor is Josh."

"Katie—"

"I'll get the money," she said shortly. She'd spent hours talking to Luke, hearing about his ex-manager, his ex-girlfriend. People he'd thought were friends. "But I'm not going to Luke. I won't allow him to think I'm after his money or that we've dragged out this investigation to earn enough for my sister's debts."

"He's not going to think that," Noah said. "He'll want to help."

"I'll get the money, Noah," she said. "Just please make sure Luke gets home safely. I'll meet him there. And you'll tell him nothing. This is personal. I'll deal with Luke my own way."

He hesitated.

"Noah, this is my decision."

Reluctantly, his expression turned grimly accepting. "Fine," he said. "But Luke's going to ask where you are."

"You'll think of something," she assured them. "I have faith in you."

"Katie—"

She started walking, needing privacy to deal with the situation her way. "I'll grab a taxi and meet you at the house." Her pace picked up. She had to escape before Luke saw her. Or maybe she was doing what Luke had accused her of too many times—running. Running from him. Running from herself. Running from caring enough to fear losing him. She'd dealt with enough loss already. And her sister was in jeopardy. It was overwhelming.

Katie hailed a cab and got in, offering her destination.

Then she dialed Ron's number. He answered on the first ring, and she went for it—she asked for the money, explained everything. He hadn't offered her the money up front before, but that's when he thought she might decline the job. Now he knew she'd stay, that she'd protect Luke.

Five minutes later, she hung up, swiping at the dampness on her cheeks, not even remembering her tears. Ron was wiring the money. He was calling Donna and arranging it. Katie fell back against the seat, emotionally exhausted. She wasn't sure she was going to be ready to face Luke tonight, but there seemed no escape.

She ran her hand through her hair and tried to calm down. Luke. She just didn't have the emotional capacity right now to do this "thing" with him. She wasn't ready. Deep down, she'd known that when she'd met his parents. She just wanted to do her job and leave, with the peace of mind of knowing that Luke was safe. She needed it to be that simple again. A job. Then she would go home.

LUKE STEPPED out of the locker room into the masses of rookie Malone's press, and silently cursed under his breath for all kinds of reasons. Malone had a chip on his shoulder as it was, and stealing his limelight, which Luke didn't want to do in the first place, wouldn't help any. Nonetheless, it was too late. The press pulled away from Malone and swarmed Luke.

"Luke! Luke!" Questions started flying faster than baseballs. He raised his hands in mock surrender. "Y'all have beaten more answers out of me tonight than the other team did bad pitches. And I threw my share of bad ones tonight."

"The scoreboard didn't show it," one of the reporters said.

"Because my team backed me up," he responded. Rick had especially done so. He'd kept more than one runner off base, but he'd also, unfortunately, taken a fly ball to the eye that had left him with a shiner and stitches to show for it. Of course, Rick had found plenty of female sympathy, which he was already exploring. A couple of blonde twins named Kari and Karra.

"Just a few more questions, Luke," a reporter said, stepping to his side. It was Tim Edwards—tall, thin, hungry for a story.

"Tim," Luke said good-naturedly. "You and I do the perpetual 'one more' question all the time, and I rarely have limits, you know that. Heck—tonight one reporter even followed me into the shower. Did I refuse to answer questions? No. All I asked for was some soap and a towel."

Laughter erupted as Luke added, with a mock salute, "Until next game. I'm going home."

Reluctantly, the crowd of media hounds let him pass and returned to their pursuit of Malone. Luke didn't have to look at Malone to know he was pissed—he could feel his hostility in the air.

But he didn't care. Katie deserved credit for getting him focused on his game tonight; he was ready to grab Katie, make a run for food and conversation, and end the night thanking her for getting his head on straight with all kinds of erotic pleasures. Before the game, she'd teased him with a bottle of whipped cream and the promise of its creative uses. What more could a man ask for? Play the game of baseball, which he loved, and then go home to a bottle of whipped cream he'd share with a woman he wasn't afraid to admit he was falling in love with.

A quick scan of the area and Luke spotted Noah and Josh, which meant Katie had to be nearby. Luke sauntered forward, feeling a rush of anticipation over seeing her that he'd never felt for a woman before. Katie had a way of keeping him smiling off the mound and, so far, focused when he was on it.

He stopped in front of Noah and Josh. "Where's Katie?" he asked, his gaze drifting up and down the concrete ramp, to find no signs of Katie. He shifted his attention back to the brothers in time to see Noah and Josh exchange an uncomfortable look, which instantly set Luke's nerves on edge. "Okay," he said. "What the hell is going on?"

"Katie went back to the house," Josh offered, another shared look with Noah. "She's meeting us there."

Luke shook his head, confused. "Did something happen? Is she okay?"

"She's fine," they both replied.

"So," he said, trying to understand and be discreet at the same time. "Is this about the 'situation' we've been dealing with?"

"It's about a situation that Katie has been dealing with on her own," Noah said, scrubbing his perpetual stubble. "A situation we have no business telling you about because it's her personal business."

Luke looked from Noah to Josh, and that punched-in-the-gut feeling intensified. He had given his trust to Katie, done so despite a past that warned him that trusting wasn't smart. If something went wrong between them, he realized suddenly, if she betrayed him, it was going to hurt like a bitch.

"You know," Luke began, and it wasn't meant to be a question, "you're going to tell me anyway."

Josh shoved his hands in his jeans pockets and rocked on his heels. "Yeah," he said. "We are."

A few minutes later, the three of them stood at the bed of Luke's truck, and Luke had gotten an earful. "Holy hell," he said, shifting his weight from one foot to the other, agitated beyond belief. Katie had kept all kinds of shit from him. The kind of stuff a woman who cares about a guy doesn't keep to herself. He'd spilled his guts to her, told her all about the hell he'd gone through. And she'd told him her own history—stories about her knee injury and losing her career. Stories of her past, he realized. Nothing that pertained to the present, though, except for a few details about starting her business.

He stared up at the pitch-black sky, the clouds shadowing the stars, kind of like his emotions were affecting his ability to think straight, and spoke half to Noah and Josh, half to himself. "I didn't even know her sister was in trouble. Not one word about this." Neither of them spoke, and he was damn thankful for that. He was trying to make sense of why Katie had kept this from him. Trying to come up with a reason other than the obvious. He simply wasn't a long-term commitment to her. He was sex and satisfaction and a job. But damn it, he wasn't going to leave her to deal with this on her own, no matter what the outcome between them. He had money. Plenty of it. Too much of it. He gave it to charities, gave it to his parents. He could give some to Katie to ensure her sister was safe. He'd seen a few guys get in deep with those kind of people. They kept coming until they got their money.

He tilted his head down, brought Noah and Josh into focus. "How much is the gambling debt?"

"Thirty total," Noah said. "It was fifty but she's already paid twenty. I'm headed to the airport as soon as I know everyone is safely where they are supposed to be," Noah added.

"The gambling problem is over, right?" Luke confirmed. They both nodded and he added, "So if I pay this, it's done?"

"It's done," Noah agreed.

"I'll give you the money," he said. "Take it and make this go away."

Josh cleared his throat. "Katie's going to be furious that we told you."

Luke pulled his keys from his pocket. "Yeah, well, I'm pissed at her for *not* telling me." He glanced at Josh. "Katie and I need some privacy to talk."

"I have your place on remote surveillance," Josh said. "I'll follow you home and stay nearby."

"Consider me gone," Noah said.

Satisfied they had an agreement in place, Luke drove them to his place.

He thought of how Katie was withdrawing now after everything they'd been through and silently cursed. If pleasure was all Katie wanted from him, if he wasn't good enough to be a confidant, a friend and lover, well, then, fine—pleasure was what he would give her.

Nothing more. Nothing less. But damn it, they were going to be honest about it. They were going to come to terms with what they were and what they were not. All she'd had to do was talk to him, and he could have taken care of her.

Almost an hour later, thanks to the after-game traffic, Luke entered the house with Noah and Josh on his heels. He took the stairs two at a time and went straight to his bedroom—their bedroom. Katie had been sharing it for over a week. They were living together, he thought. Living together and he didn't know what was going on in her life.

He found her clothes in a pile on the bathroom floor, her swimsuit missing from the towel rack, which meant she was in the pool—her replacement for running since hurting her knee. He went back down the stairs, and Noah and Josh were nowhere in sight. Smart. Good. They knew when to get lost. Noah'd pack and be gone without saying a word.

In all of sixty seconds, Luke had made his way to the sliding glass doors, and sure enough, they were un-latched, indicating Katie was out back. He took the brick path lined with shrubs and flowers, and found the long, eight-ball-shaped pool, and Katie in the midst of laps.

Luke considered his options, frustration still churn-ing inside him. He decided the best way to talk to Katie was naked. That seemed to be how they communicated best. And if this was all about pleasure for her, then, by God, let there be pleasure.

12

LUKE WAS STANDING at the end of the pool, buck naked and about to dive into the pool, when Katie seemed to sense his presence. She reached the edge of the water and grabbed the wall, blinking up at him. "Luke?" she murmured, sounding surprised, her eyes lingering below the waist before lifting back to his face, her expression tentative, as if she seemed to sense his hostility. "Where are Noah and Josh?"

"Not important," he said, diving into the water. He was behind her in a matter of seconds, pinning her against the wall, his front to her back. He pressed his cheek to hers. "Let's not waste any time," he said, and tugged her bottoms down her legs. His palms skimmed a path over her hips and raised her above the water to lightly smack one perfect, round cheek. She gasped with a mixture of surprise and pleasure.

"Luke," she whispered, in the midst of a moan as he slid his hand along the crevice of her backside. That perfect, round backside. Damn, he loved her ass.

"I want you, Katie," he said. "I always want you." *As insane as that might be,* he thought.

"What's wrong with you?" she demanded.

"Why does me wanting you mean something is wrong?" He untied her top, removed it and tossed it into the water, as well. He held her close, pressed his lips to her ear. "I'm trying to give you what you want, Katie. Pleasure without questions. Pleasure without commitment."

He tweaked her nipples and she protested. "I've never said such a thing. Never."

"It's what you didn't say."

"I don't know what you're talking about," she vowed breathlessly, but the denial didn't keep her from arching against him.

"I told you this is what you wanted," he said, his teeth scraping her shoulder, hand flattening on her stomach, and then lower, as he played with her clit.

She stiffened. "What I want is for you to stop acting like the jerk you were the day I met you," she hoarsely demanded.

He froze, his gut twisted with the impact of her words. She was right. He was being a jerk and hadn't meant to.

This hadn't been his plan when he'd come home, when he came outside. But for the first time since Ron had forced their introduction, Luke was pushing her away. He was trying to upset her because it was easier than dealing with what she might make him feel. What she'd already made him feel—betrayed and hurt. In other words, he was doing exactly what she'd been doing.

He backed off her immediately. "You want to know what's wrong?"

"Yes!" she exclaimed. "Yes. I want to know what is wrong."

He heaved a breath. Looked away. Once he asked this question, he had to live with her answer. An answer that might change everything between them. Or then again, maybe it would make things crystal clear. He wanted crystal clear. He fixed her in his stare, made his demand. "Why didn't you come to me about your sister's situation? Why didn't you let me help?"

Shock flooded her face. "I... Luke." Her lips pursed. "Ron told you."

"Ron knew?" he demanded, his gut clenching. "Everyone knew but me, Katie?" He was beyond himself. "I thought we had something good going on here, but I'm completely shut out."

Emotion flashed across her face, darkening her eyes. "I didn't want you to think I was like the other people around you," she said finally. "That I wanted something from you."

Anger churned through him. "Bullshit, Katie," he said. "At least have the courage to be honest about what you feel."

She shoved on his unmoving chest. "Let me by."

Not a chance in hell. "Not until you talk to me."

"Talk?" she blurted fiercely. "You want to talk? How about this, Luke. I didn't want your help! Why can't you accept that? I talked to Ron. He gave me an advance. The situation is handled. Done. There is nothing more to tell."

Luke could barely believe his ears. "You asked Ron for help, but not me?"

"Yes!" she said. "Yes, I asked Ron and not you." She

shoved one more time on his chest. "Let me go, Luke."
When he didn't budge, her features turned stormy.
"Damn you, Luke. I can't do this thing with you. I can't
do the caring, sharing, falling-in-love stuff. I can't. I
won't. That wasn't the deal. That isn't what we were
doing."

He ignored the rejection, focused on the inadvertent
admission. "You're falling in love with me?"

She squeezed her eyes shut. "Why are you doing
this?"

He moved his hands to the side of her face. "Because
I'm falling in love with you, Katie."

She sucked in a breath and blinked up at him, water
clinging to her dark lashes, her brown eyes troubled. "I
don't want to feel these things."

His chest tightened at what he saw in her face, what
he sensed behind her words—she'd lost her parents.
"I'm afraid of losing you, too," he said.

She shook her head. "You don't understand."

"I do," he said softly. "I remember what you told me
about your parents, Katie. I know you're worried about
your sister. I know that asshole Joey screwed you over. I
know you're scared. But we can get through it together.
I can't promise something won't happen to me. No one
can make that kind of promise. I can't even promise
I'll never be a jerk again, like when I jumped in the
pool. But I *can* promise I will try and make every day
we spend together memorable." He pressed their palms
together. "We're good together, Katie. Damn good. I
don't want to lose that. I don't want to lose us."

"Luke," she whispered, staring down at their palms
for long seconds before her fingers entwined with his

and closed down. Slowly, her gaze lifted. "I don't want to lose us, either. Kiss me, Luke."

His lips brushed hers, tongue moving past her lips in a gentle probe, a sweet caress, before he said, "I'm going to kiss you again. And again. I'm going to kiss every last inch of you. And then I'm going to start over and do it again."

She smiled against his mouth. "What are you waiting for?"

HOURS LATER, in Luke's bedroom, Katie and Luke lay together, naked, talking. She ran her hand over his chest, through the springy hair she loved so much. "I should be furious that you gave Josh that money."

He leaned up, looked at her. "Come again?"

She rotated around to face him, onto her stomach, teasing him. "I'm not some kept woman, you know."

"Oh, believe me," he said, "I know."

She smiled. "What's that supposed to mean?"

"It means you are the most independent, stubborn woman I have ever known."

"Back at ya, mister," she said.

"Hey, hey," he said. "Are you calling me a woman?"

She laughed. He made her laugh so easily. After everything she'd felt today—all the emotions, the fear— Luke still made her smile. She climbed on top of him, straddling him, his heated stare warming her body. Katie leaned down and kissed him. "You are more man than any man I've ever dated."

His hand slid to her face. "Then let me have all the woman, Katie. Don't shut me out again." And in true

Luke form, he didn't demand she respond. Instead, he kissed her, a soft, gentle kiss that reminded her, yet again, why she was falling in love with him. Why she probably already was in love with him. And why she had to take a chance that she might lose him in order to ever fully have him.

A WEEK LATER, the final at-home game before a month on the road had ended in a loss. Luke walked toward the locker room, his elbow wrapped with an Ace bandage, a bouncing ball having found him perfectly. To his right was Rick, to his left Conn, who stalked several steps ahead of them, pissed off as hell at Malone. "Son of a bitch," Conn mumbled. "Ignored every other hand signal." His voice raised. "Do you know what a hand signal is?"

Malone turned around and shot the finger at Conn. "Here's a hand signal for you."

"You shit," Conn muttered, his New York accent getting stronger, which was never a good sign. "You just wait until you get into that locker room. I'll show ya hand signals."

"Oh, man," Rick mumbled under his breath. "I'll warn Coach."

"He's not worth a brawl that might end badly," Luke warned, double-stepping to Conn's side.

"For him," Conn said. "It's going to end bad *for him.* He needs a lesson in humility, and I'm the man to give it to him."

By the time they hit the locker-room door, Coach was in between Conn and Malone, and he waved off the press, sealing the locker room. Luke knew when to get lost, and this was one of those times. He went to his locker, undressed, heading to the shower for a fast escape, Coach mediating the shouting match behind him.

Fifteen minutes later, he and Rick were both dressed, about to shut their lockers and head out, when the fight broke out. Conn and Malone were on top of each other. Luke cursed and moved to the side where Malone crashed against the lockers a few inches from where Luke had stood. The next thing Luke knew, his bag was on the ground, and Malone was on top of it.

The team gathered in observation, with shouts of encouragement and otherwise, all vocalized loudly. Rick cursed and grabbed Conn by the shirt. Luke used his good arm and yanked Malone off his duffel. And that was when it happened. The syringes fell out of his bag.

Malone grabbed one and stood up. Coach rounded the corner. Malone held up the syringe and shook it in the air. "Is this how you manage that fast pitch?" he challenged Luke. "With drugs?"

The room went silent. Luke's eyes latched on to Malone's, and Luke knew in his gut that Malone had done this. Luke's heartbeat pounded in his ears, his gaze lifting to where Coach stood. Malone was a sick bastard. The kid had problems, and Luke had been too busy dealing with his stalker to see that. Now he was paying the price and so might his career.

"Drug test me now, Coach," Luke said, his spine stiff. "Because I can promise you, I won't fail. Those are not my syringes or my drugs. I've been set up."

IN A PINK SATIN ROBE, with a can of whipped cream in hand, Katie went in search of Luke. She found him sitting exactly where expected—on the leather sofa in the den watching *SportsCenter,* just as one of the commentators speculated about his use of steroids and how he might have beaten the drug test.

For days now, he'd tortured himself watching his own press, grumbling that Carl Malone had set him up, which was true, she had no doubt. And they were watching him, waiting for him to screw up.

Katie loved Luke too much to allow him to wallow in self-pity, she knew that now. There was no denying it. She loved the way he talked, the way he walked, the way he drank from her cup without asking. She loved him. That meant she needed to take care of him, as he had taken care of her the other night after her panic attack over her sister, who was, thankfully, out of trouble. No more loan sharks. No more danger. So Katie was armed and ready to take action. She'd stop at nothing to get Luke's mind off his troubles. She was a woman on a mission.

Tilting her chin up, she marched into the den, rounded the couch and went straight to the television, not bothering to reach for the remote. It was in his hand where it stayed. Instead, she hit the manual button and turned it off.

"Hey!" he started to complain. "I was—"

Katie dropped the robe. She was naked underneath. "No more *SportsCenter,*" she said. She held up the whipped cream. "I bought this almost two weeks ago, and we never used it. Remember?"

He tossed the remote to the floor. "No more *SportsCenter.*"

She smiled and ripped the top off the whipped cream and sprayed it on her nipples. "Would you like to help me decorate?" she asked, crossing the small space between them and straddling him. "Or just lick off my handiwork?"

"Both," he said, his hands closing around her waist as his tongue twirled the whipped cream around her nipple. "More, please."

She pointed to the opposite nipple. "This one first."

A smile touched his lips a moment before it touched the whipped cream on her other breast. She sprayed more, on her nipples, between them. Lower. She planned on going much lower.

"Stand up, baby," he urged. "Let me decorate my favorite little V."

"Katie! Luke!" It was Noah.

"Oh, my God!" Katie said, and tried to scramble away.

Luke licked her nipple clean. "I'll hurry."

"Katie! Luke!" Noah's voice got closer.

"Let go, Luke!" Luke chuckled and freed her. Katie scrambled for her robe, pulled it on. "Why is it I am always scrambling to get my clothes on around you?" she asked, tying her robe not a second too soon.

Noah appeared in the doorway and charged toward them. "Josh was right," he said, crossing the room. "He—" His eyebrows dipped as he looked at Katie. "What's all over you?" His eyes went wide. "Is that whipped cream?" He started to laugh, his gaze spotting the can on the couch. "It's whipped cream."

Katie crossed her arms in front of her body. "Just tell us what you came to tell us."

"Malone was at a junior college before UT," he said. "His major was…get this…forensic science. And backtracking, we now know the letters started right after he was picked up on the roster, right before he arrived, which deflected attention from him."

Katie's eyes went wide. "So he knew how to write those letters and not get caught."

"That's right," Noah said. "And he had some emotional issues in high school. His dad was an alcoholic, hit his mom. Malone was competitive, started fights. Apparently, baseball got him straight. He was the leader of the team, the star player and that seemed to settle him down. Or so everyone thought. He fixated on Luke for reasons I am not sure we will ever understand." He sat on the arm of the couch. "Oh, and I know how he got into the house and cleared the security feed."

"How?" Luke and Katie asked at the same moment.

"Jessica," he said. "Josh saw her at one of the games acting funny. Apparently, she went to all the games. Somehow Malone met her and used her to get to you. He's been dating her. Using her. Whatever you want to call it. She's at his house now."

"That low-life bastard," Luke said. "That sorry, low-life bastard." He was visibly seething. "That's it. I've had enough." He charged forward, heading toward the door.

"Where are you going, Luke?" Katie demanded, running after him, trying to grab his arm despite a gaping robe and whipped cream all over her.

"Luke," Noah called, in pursuit, as well. They followed him to the kitchen and then to the hallway. "Hold up, man. I'm putting together evidence. The police will handle this when the time is right."

"The time is right," Luke said. "Call them. Tell them to meet me there."

"Luke!" Katie cried, this time getting a grip on his arm. "At least let me get dressed. Let me come with you."

He pried her fingers from his arm. "This is between me and Malone, Katie. I'm doing this myself."

"This is between Malone and the police," Noah corrected.

"Right," Luke said, reaching the front door. "Me, Malone and the police. Call them." He yanked open the door and exited.

Katie cast Noah a desperate look. "Please! Go after him. I'll meet you there." She started for the stairs as Noah headed toward the door, her stomach twisting in knots, instincts in play. She stopped. "Noah!" He turned back to her. "Do what Luke said. Call the police." She didn't wait for a response. She darted up the stairs. She had another one of those gut feelings her father had said to never ignore. This wasn't going to end well.

13

LUKE WAS already driving before he realized he didn't have Malone's address, but a call to a team assistant proved effective. He pulled in to the driveway of the stucco, beachside house and barely had the truck in Park before he was out the door.

He'd thought about beating Malone's ass as soon as he'd gotten into the truck, but he'd calmed down enough since then to realize that wasn't going to do anything but hurt his career. And Malone had already done enough of that. But he owed it to Maria to get Jessica out of Malone's place before the police and the press arrived. As disappointed as he was in Jessica's role in all this, she was a kid, manipulated by a creep.

He took the short set of stairs in a flying leap and rang the doorbell over and over. Then he started pounding on the door until it flew open. Malone stood there in no shirt, bare feet and jeans. "What are you doing here, Winter?"

"I know everything. The letters. The planted drugs. Everything, you son of a bitch. And you know what? It's between you and me—I want Jessica out of here."

Her car wasn't in the driveway, but Noah had said she was here, and Luke believed him.

Malone made a wacko motion at the side of his head and whistled. "You are truly going off the deep end. Losing it big-time, Luke."

"Jessica!" Luke yelled, and then refocused on Malone. "I want her out of this. It's between you and me, let's leave it that way."

"Luke?"

"Jessica," he called. "It's time to go home. Get your things."

Malone tried to shut the door. Luke caught it with his hand and foot. "She's leaving," he said. "You're a pathetic man. Using a kid like this." He raised his voice. "Come on, Jessica! You're going home."

"She's not going anywhere with you," Malone said. "Get lost, Luke. Inject your steroids or whatever you need to do to get through the day."

"Let me by, Carl!" Jessica said. "Let me by. Luke... I'm sorry, Luke. I...I... Let me pass, Carl!"

Luke and Malone glared at each other. "Let her go, Malone." Malone looked as if he was going to refuse, but suddenly jerked back and opened the door.

Jessica raced toward Luke. "Go to the truck," he ordered brusquely, right as Noah pulled his rented sedan to a skidding halt in the driveway, shoved open the door and got out.

"Everything okay, Luke?" Noah shouted.

Luke eyed the doorway. Malone had disappeared inside. He turned to address Noah. "I'm taking Jessica home before the police get here," he called a moment before a blast hit his back as Malone rammed him from behind in a powerful burst of force that sent him tumbling down the concrete stairs in a roll. He bounced down on his right side, his pitching arm underneath him. Pain exploded along his shoulder, through his arm, and he heard the bone snap a moment before his head hit the pavement and he blacked out.

KATIE ARRIVED at Malone's place to find two police cars and an ambulance at the front of the house. Nausea rushed over her, fear tightening her chest. Luke. She knew that ambulance was for Luke. Her mind was spinning, fingers going numb. Dizzy with her reaction, she still managed to thrust the car door open—not even bothering to shut it behind her—and started to run toward the ambulance.

Noah greeted her halfway there.

"It's Luke, isn't it?" she demanded, grabbing his arm for support. She could not lose Luke, too. She couldn't.

"He has a concussion, and he broke his arm," he said. "His pitching arm, Katie. It's a bad break."

He was alive. "But he's okay," she confirmed. "He's going to be okay?"

"You might have a hard time convincing him of that," Noah said. "But yes."

Katie would convince him he was okay. He was alive, and he was going to stay that way. That was what mattered. She started running, rounding the back of the ambulance right before they shut the door, barely blinking at the sight of Malone in cuffs standing next to one of the police cars.

She brought the back of the ambulance into focus.

"Luke!" He was on the gurney, his arm splinted, his head bandaged.

"Katie," he whispered, and tried to sit up.

The EMT pressed him back down. "Don't move." The worker motioned her forward.

Katie rushed inside and sat beside him, on the opposite side of the bed from the emergency worker. She touched his face, her chest tight with emotion. "You have no idea how scared I was when I saw the ambulance."

He tried to smile but couldn't. "Ah," he said. "My head."

"Concussion," the EMT told her. "He blacked out for about five minutes."

"How bad?" Katie asked, eyeing the monitor they had attached to him, thankful it wasn't buzzing with alerts. He appeared stable.

"I have a hard…head," Luke whispered hoarsely.

"We won't know until they do tests at the hospital," was the EMT's official answer.

The ambulance started moving. Katie bent down and kissed him. "I love you, Luke," she said. "I love you so much. You and your hard head."

"Katie," he whispered, shutting his eyes. "I…am not sure I will pitch again. I…don't know what that means for me."

"You will pitch again," she said, sensing the torment in him. "You will. They'll fix your arm."

His lashes lifted just barely, as if he couldn't get the energy to raise them all the way. "Is that what they told you about…your knee?"

Her heart squeezed with that question because, yes, that was what they'd told her. They'd told her she would dance again. Katie wasn't going to do that to him. She took his hand. "Whatever happens, Luke, I'm here for you." He didn't respond.

His lashes lowered again and Katie looked at the EMT.

"I gave him some pain medicine," he said. "He's sleeping."

So he didn't hear her vow. She'd tell him again when he woke up. She'd tell him however many times he needed to hear it. No one had been there for her when she'd lost her dancing. If Luke lost pitching, if he lost baseball, she wasn't going to let it destroy him.

LUKE WOKE to find Katie asleep in the green hospital chair beside his bed where she'd dozed off and on through all the poking and prodding he'd been through. He stared at her, the woman he loved. Pale, perfect skin, smudged with dark circles. Not a stitch of makeup. Her dark hair fell wildly around her face, a rubber band at the back of her neck barely holding it in place. And she was the most beautiful woman he'd ever seen. She'd been through so much, and she deserved happiness. He had thought he could give her that happiness. He had thought he would be the man to make her wake up and smile every day. But now—well, the man she thought she knew, the man he knew himself to be, might *not be* anymore.

"Going to Malone's house was such an idiotic move," Luke mumbled under his breath, staring out the hospital window as he waited for the specialist to tell him his future.

"I told you to stop second-guessing yourself," Katie

whispered, obviously awake when he'd thought she was sleeping. She sat up and stretched.

Glancing at the clock, he noted it was midafternoon, almost three o'clock. They'd been at the hospital since midnight the night before.

Katie pushed to her feet and walked to his side. Ran her hand over his face. "No news is better than bad news." Her voice was comforting. A light in the darkness.

Male voices sounded in the hallway before Rick and Josh appeared. "We snuck in pizza," Rick said. "We couldn't let you wallow in hospital food." He rolled the table in front of the bed and opened the box. "We'd have brought beer if we thought it wouldn't get us kicked out."

Luke scooted to a sitting position and shoved the table aside. "I'll eat later," he said. "Right now, I'll settle for either the doctor's prognosis or maybe Malone's head on a stick."

"That you can have," Josh said, ignoring the pizza, as well, and leaning against the wall. "He admitted to everything. The letters, planting the drugs, even paying a water boy to put salt in the canister during practice."

Luke digested that with less satisfaction than he would have under different circumstances.

"I checked on Jessica while you were sleeping," Katie interjected. "Her mom is pretty upset. There was a lot of Spanish yelling that went on—I'm pretty sure Jessica will get all the attention and advice she needs from her mother."

Everyone laughed because they'd all heard Maria's

Spanish exclamations. "I'd hate to be Jessica right about now," Rick said, laughing, before motioning to Luke. "Coach said he'd be by tomorrow after you have time to recover a little more."

"You mean after he knows if I'm going to be able to pitch anymore," Luke said. Two of his doctors came into the room: Dr. Reyes, an orthopedic specialist with gray hair and a trim, medium build; and Dr. Willis, a forty-something neurosurgeon with dark hair and a mustache. Luke was pretty sure two for one was not a good sign.

"Can we please be alone with Luke?" Dr. Willis asked.

"Sure thing, Doc," Rick said, moving toward the door. Josh quickly followed.

Katie went to Luke's side and kissed his cheek. "I'll be nearby when you need me."

Luke grabbed her hand. "Stay." She glanced at the doctors, who nodded their acceptance.

Thirty minutes later, Luke was about to be rolled down the hall for more testing, and Katie would have to stay behind. He had a twenty-five percent chance of full recovery. In other words, he wasn't likely to pitch again.

"If you want to play ball, Luke," she said, "fight for it. Screw the odds."

"Is that what you did?" he asked. "Did you fight for it?"

She shook her head. "No," she said. "And I regret it. Don't regret, Luke." She squeezed his hand and then let it go, and they rolled him away. Somehow, he felt as if he was leaving her behind forever when she was simply down the hall from him. It was a feeling that ground through his gut and wouldn't let go.

KATIE WATCHED Luke disappear through a set of double doors, exhaustion tearing her down. Worry for Luke was worse than the exhaustion.

Ron stepped by her side. "Go home, Katie," he said.

"Nice to see you, too, Ron. Aren't you going to ask how he is?"

"Bad," he said. "I know. I talked to the doctors. I'm here now." He repeated his order, "Go home, Katie."

She shook off the suggestion. "Noah is bringing me a change of clothes," she said. "I'm staying."

"No," he said. "I mean go back to New York. The job is done."

She blinked, turned to him. "What?"

"Luke has a tough path ahead of him, and he has to focus. Not on you. On him. On his career. If you think he can do that with you around, you're wrong. He'll worry about you accepting him. He'll worry about you, not him."

"I…" She shut her mouth on the objection. Ron was right. Luke would worry about her. He was always worried about her. The glory of Luke was that he wasn't a self-centered egomaniac. She tried to breathe but couldn't seem to fill her lungs. The idea of leaving him all but killed her. Didn't he need her? "I'll talk to him."

Ron shook his head. "No, Katie. You talk to him and you'll both convince yourselves that you staying is the

right move. Let him get well. Let him be about baseball."
He studied her. "Do you love him?"

"Yes," she said. "Yes. I love him."

"Then walk away."

She stared down that hallway, to the empty space
where Luke had been only a minute before. She pressed
her hands to her face and tried to fight the tears. She'd
lost her dancing. Her dream. Her life. She couldn't be
the reason Luke lost baseball.

14

THREE MONTHS and Luke still couldn't walk through his own house without memories of Katie punching him in the gut. Right when he thought he'd recovered, it would happen again. Like now. Luke poured a cup of coffee and turned toward the kitchen table, and the memory sped at him like a bullet. Katie naked on top of that counter, legs wide, him between them. The kisses. The passion. The moans.

"Damn it," he cursed, pressing his fingers to the bridge of his nose. Why did he keep doing this? He wasn't an idiot. He wasn't a loser. Not even without his pitching arm. Katie had left without so much as a good-bye, deserted him in his hour of need. And proved she wasn't what he thought she was. Her "I love you, Luke" in that ambulance had either been a hallucination from his head injury or a bunch of crap. So why couldn't he get her out of his head? Why did he feel as if he was missing something he shouldn't be missing?

The doorbell rang and he let Maria answer it. He was in a foul mood this morning. Again. The *again* being Maria's opinion. That wasn't true. He was now in a fine mood after his morning coffee. It was simply a new routine. Wake up and be foul like the rest of the world. Drink coffee and perk up. He kind of liked it, too. And as much as he missed pitching, the morning coffee and no-pressure-to-perform thing wouldn't be so bad if he had the slightest clue about what he was going to do with the rest of his life.

He sat down at the kitchen table, away from the television and freaking *SportsCenter*. He didn't want to hear about baseball. Or football. Or even flipping volleyball. Whatever he did was not going to have anything to do with sports. Everyone expected him to be involved with sports. Open a bar. Hang all kinds of sports crap on the walls. No. Bar.

"Luke." It was Ron. "How's it going?"

"Thinking about opening a bar. You know. Sticking sports crap on the walls. Build-it-and-they-will-come kind of thing." He lifted his out-of-date newspaper with the crossword puzzle he'd been doing for well over a week. "And I'm looking for a four-letter word for *ass*. Any ideas. And don't say Luke."

Ron stared at him and then said, "I'd say *mule*. But then again, I hear Rick is dating Libby again."

Luke snorted and grabbed his pencil. "Rick, it is." He tossed his pencil down and leaned back in his chair to study Ron over his coffee cup. "What's on your mind?"

"A coaching job," he said.

"And here I thought management was your forte," Luke quipped. "We've had this conversation. I don't want to be stuck in a tie commentating sporting events on some news channel. And *I don't* want to coach the sport I wish I was playing." He irritably tapped his fingers on his mug.

"Not even if you'd be coaching in New York?"

Luke felt the tension spiral down his spine. "Why would I want to go to New York?"

"Because I sent her away, Luke. I told her she would distract you. I told her you couldn't fight your injury and would worry about pleasing her. I pushed her to leave and I pushed her hard."

Luke set his coffee mug down, liquid slopping over the sides. "When?"

"While you were having your tests," he replied. "At the hospital. It was the right thing to do, Luke. I am your manager, and—"

"Were," Luke said, standing up. "*Were* my manager."

Ron reached in his pocket and slid a card onto the table. "If you want the job, I believe it can be yours. They want you bad."

IT WAS Saturday and Katie blinked awake to the rumbling of thunder, rain splattering on the windows of her New York apartment. She tugged her white down comforter to her chin as the memory of another storm assailed her. She'd been in Luke's kitchen when he'd come home from practice, a storm rolling in that had set the mood for the stormy encounter they'd shared, the passion that had followed.

She snuggled down in the blankets and covered her head with her pillow. She was definitely going back to sleep. And waking up when it was nice and sunny. "Rain, rain, go away," she murmured.

Rolling to her side, she tucked the pillow under her head and pounded it. Promised herself she'd stop thinking about Luke. He hated her, she was sure. And with good reason. She should never have listened to Ron and left Luke. And now he wasn't playing ball. He'd lost baseball, and she hadn't been there to help him get through it. But she'd made her decision. She had to live with it.

"Grr," she muttered into the pillow. She wasn't going to be able to sleep. She tossed aside the covers, shoved her feet to the floor. She was up but she wasn't getting dressed. Boxers, a tank top, coffee and a book. That would be her new thunderstorm memory. A nice, relaxing, peaceful day.

She started the coffeepot, and then washed her face and brushed her teeth. Scanning her bookshelf, she chose a thriller, a scary story to fit the weather.

A glimpse in her full-length vanity mirror drew a grimace. Donna was right. She was skinny. She hadn't been eating. For a moment, she contemplated stepping on the scale, but then decided against it. She didn't want to know. She'd eat. Lunch. Later.

With coffee and book in hand, she headed back to bed and the expensive, snuggly, down comforter she'd bought on a whim and never regretted. She had managed to get through page one of her book when her cell phone jangled on the nightstand. She considered ignoring it. Her sister was fine, even dating a nice, respectable doctor. A real change from her ex.

She snatched up the phone and noted the caller ID—Donna, of course. She answered. "Hello."

"Turn on ESPN," Donna ordered.

"Are you going to say hello?" Katie asked, rolling her eyes.

"Do it!" Donna demanded.

Katie sighed and grabbed the remote, also on the nightstand, and did as she'd been told. "Cable's out," she said. "What can possibly be so urgent on ESPN? Because if you want me to ogle some guy's backside, I have to tell you, I prefer the novel I just started."

"Oh, you want to ogle this backside, honey," Donna said. "Guess who just took a coaching job with the New York Comets?"

Katie sat up, tossed her book aside. "Luke?"

"That's right, sweetheart, and he's in town," she said. "ESPN interviewed him live here this morning."

Her doorbell rang. "Someone's at my door. I... You think? No. No. It can't be." It rang again. "I have to go." She hung up and tossed the phone onto the bed. "It can't be him."

Katie started for the door, but stopped. She wasn't dressed. Robe. She needed a robe. She grabbed the one at the back of the bathroom door, and made the mistake of looking in the mirror. Cringing, she reasoned, "It's not him anyway."

Whoever had been ringing the doorbell was now knocking. She pressed her hands to the door and forced herself to calm down. "Who is it?"

Silence. "Katie, it's Luke."

She couldn't seem to find her voice. And she tried. She tried so damn hard. She gave up and yanked the door open. "I... Luke." He was as gorgeous as ever, maybe thinner by a few pounds. His hair a little longer than she remembered, curled a bit over his brow. "You look good." She thought of that image of herself in the mirror. "I was in bed."

He smiled.

"I mean. Reading. I was reading in…"

He arched a brow. "Bed?"

What was she supposed to say? *Care to join me?* Of course he wouldn't. Not after all that had happened between them. She stepped back to allow him entry. "Come in."

He stepped into the room, inspecting her little apartment, which was about the size of his kitchen and den and nothing more. He still had that sexy Texas saunter that made his nice, tight backside oh, so drool worthy. She shut the door and leaned against it. "I have coffee. You want coffee?"

"Coffee sounds great," he said.

She rushed to her sparkling, all-white kitchen and grabbed a coffee cup. When she was done, she set his mug on the counter. He took a sip. "You remember how I like it."

She remembered a lot of things. Couldn't forget, no matter how hard she tried. They stood there at her kitchen counter and stared at each other, and Katie was melting. Melting and she didn't know what to do about it.

"I just heard congratulations are in order. You're coaching. That's wonderful, Luke. Really wonderful." She studied him. "Is it wonderful to you, Luke? Are you happy about it?"

"I think it has the potential to be wonderful," he said after a short pause.

"Good. That's good."

"I've missed you, Katie."

Her heart squeezed. "I've missed you, too, Luke." She wanted to explain about leaving, but she didn't know how, and wasn't sure she should.

"Ron told me why you left," he said.

She swallowed hard. "He did?"

He nodded. "Now you tell me."

"Because I didn't want to distract you. Because I didn't want you to lose baseball. Because…" Emotion welled in her chest. "Because I was an idiot to ever listen to that man. You lost baseball anyway, and I wasn't there to help you get through it. But you did. I'm glad you did."

He didn't move, didn't immediately respond. "I'm not through it, Katie. Some days, I'm hanging by a string. But I'm trying. I'm getting there." Thunder rumbled again, shaking the windows. "The rain makes me think of that day—"

"In your kitchen," she said softly, awareness fluttering in her stomach, sexy images of them making love teasing her mind. "I woke up thinking about it this morning."

His eyes warmed. "What if I told you I could have coached in Los Angeles, but I came here for you? So you could be close to your sister and I could be close to you."

Her heart tripped and then raced. "How close, Luke?" she asked. "How close do you want to be?"

He stepped forward, stopping just short of touching her. "In the same bed," he said, his voice low, sensual, full of the erotic promise of the past. "Reading a book by your side—for the rest of my life, Katie." Finally, he reached for her, the touch charging through her senses, pure bliss, like coming home when she'd been lost.

"I love you, too, Luke," she said, slipping into his arms. "I love you so much. It destroyed me to leave you."

"I'm here now," he promised. "And I'm here to stay."

"Kiss me," she ordered, hungry for a taste of him. "Kiss me and then let's go to bed and sleep all day."

"Sleep?" he challenged.

She cast him a mischievous smile. "That's code for *pass the whipped cream, please.*"

* * * * *

COMING NEXT MONTH

Available August 31, 2010

HBCNM0810

REQUEST YOUR FREE BOOKS!

2 FREE NOVELS PLUS 2 FREE GIFTS!

HARLEQUIN® *Blaze*

Red-hot reads!

HB10R

HARLEQUIN®

A Romance

FOR EVERY MOOD™

Spotlight on

— Heart & Home —

Heartwarming romances
where love can happen
right when you least expect it.

See the next page to enjoy a sneak peek
from Harlequin Superromance®,
a Heart and Home series.

Police chief Juliette Tremblant recognized the shape of the man strolling down the street—in as calm and leisurely fashion as if it were the middle of the day rather than midnight. She slowed her car, convinced her eyes were playing tricks on her. It had been a long time since Tyler O'Neill had been seen in this town.

As she pulled to a stop at the curb, he turned toward her, and her heart about stopped.

"What the hell are you doing here, Tyler?"

"Well, if it isn't Juliette Tremblant." He made his way over to her, then leaned down so he could look her in the eye. He was close enough to touch.

Juliette was not, repeat, *not* going to touch Tyler O'Neill. Not with her fingers. Not with a ten-foot pole. There would be no touching. Which was too bad, since it was the only way she was ever going to convince herself the man standing in front of her—as rumpled and heart-stoppingly handsome now as he'd been at sixteen—was real.

And not a figment of all her furious revenge dreams.

"What are you doing back in Bonne Terre?" she asked.

"The manor is sitting empty," Tyler said and shrugged, as though his arriving out of the blue after ten years was casual. "Seems like someone should be watching over the family home."

"You?" She laughed at the very notion of him being here for any unselfish reason. "Please."

He stared at her for a second, then smiled. Her heart fluttered against her chest—a small mechanical bird powered by that smile.

"You're right." But that cryptic comment was all he offered.

Juliette bit her lip against the other questions.

Why did you go?

Why didn't you write? Call?

What did I do?

But what would be the point? Ten years of silence were all the answer she really needed.

She had sworn off feeling anything for this man long ago. Yet one look at him and all the old hurt and rage resurfaced as though they'd been waiting for the chance. That made her mad.

She put the car in gear, determined not to waste another minute thinking about Tyler O'Neill. "Have a good night, Tyler," she said, liking all the cool "go screw yourself" she managed to fit into those words.

It seems Juliette has an old score to settle with Tyler.
Pick up TYLER O'NEILL'S REDEMPTION
to see how he makes it up to her.
Available September 2010,
only from Harlequin Superromance.